CREDIT-CARD
CAROLE

CREDIT-CARD CAROLE

SHEILA SOLOMON KLASS

CHARLES SCRIBNER'S SONS · NEW YORK

Copyright © 1987 by Sheila Solomon Klass

Charles Scribner's Sons Books for Young Readers
Macmillan Publishing Company
866 Third Avenue, New York, NY 10022
Collier Macmillan Canada, Inc.

Printed in the United States of America
First Edition
10 9 8 7 6 5 4 3 2 1

Library of Congress Cataloging-in-Publication Data
Klass, Sheila Solomon.   Credit-card Carole.
    Summary: When her father's decision to quit his lucrative job to "find himself" as an actor changes their family's finances, pampered sixteen-year-old Carole is dismayed that she must give up her credit card and get a job herself.
    [1. Money—Fiction] I. Title.
PZ7.K67814Cr 1987   [Fic]   87-9863
ISBN 0-684-18889-9

For Larry Wolff, with love
and appreciation for Benjamin
and much much more

Imagine a normal father who is forty-two years old, a bookworm, sensible, a successful dentist, short and slim with a young Walter Matthau kind of face, a dentist with a light-as-a-feather touch, his patients say. Imagine that this Dr. Tooth blows his circuits. Without any warning one afternoon he announces that he is about to "Fly after the bluebird of happiness! Have a rendezvous with destiny! Chase rainbows!" I quote him exactly, the denture-dreamer, the poet of plaque. Do I sound bitter? Let me tell you, I *was* bitter.

On the very day Brutal Blake, my English teacher, spent a whole period explaining the term *irony*—a turn of events contrary to what you expect—I came home from school to find the cushions knocked out from under my all-American life.

1

Irony? You bet.

If I wrote about this to Dr. Joyce Brothers and my letter got printed, about a million readers would write in saying Carole Warren is a humungous liar. She doesn't know what she's talking about. She's been brainwashed. Money is what life is all about, money and buying whatever you want, eating out—Italian, Chinese, Mexican—having a good stereo and records and tapes, and a VCR and a Walkman, and shopping for whatever you like at Bloomie's or The Gap, and phoning anywhere and talking as long as you please. That's living.

Well, they'd be wrong. Money is what life is about but not all about. That's not living. That's spending. And I can understand where they're at because I was there myself not long ago. Credit-Card Carole, that's me.

CHAPTER

1

It was an ordinary Thursday afternoon in Ashland, New Jersey, suburbia, USA. My friend, Jim Dunham, was walking me part of the way home. The most exciting thing in town was the fall foliage, flame-colored and lemon and orange. It was the kind of day that brought out all the senior citizens with their straw brooms in hand so they could sweep the walks and talk to folks. Three elderly ladies on different streets said "Afternoon" to us and pointed out the lovely colors, the exquisite Ashland leaves, the picture-postcard fall.

Ashland is famous all over Bergen County for the following remarkable features: no undertakers, no taverns, nine beauty salons, and lots of trees. The last neighbor who greeted us, Mrs. Monroe from around the corner, whom I've known ever since I was a kid, insisted that a branch of yellows go with me. "'A thing of beauty is a joy forever,'" she said. Mrs. Monroe is a nice old lady always quoting, as if every deep thought she ever had was said better by someone else. "Carry the beauty indoors," she ordered.

Jim, ever the gentleman, took it from her and carried it for me. He's tall, blond wavy hair, gray eyes, very thin. He's the worst-dressed kid in Ashland High School though his family is one of the richest in town. He was wearing his usual: old jogging shoes, faded jeans, and a worn white shirt with buttons missing. With him shabbiness is a matter of pride.

As we went along, we continued an old hassle. It had to do with motives, Jim's favorite subject. It wasn't an angry argument, just a permanent difference of opinion. We were coming from afterschool activities. He had been practicing his cello in the music room while I ran on the track. He was bugging me about running.

Running is the most exhilarating activity of my life. When I run there is only wind and earth and speed—and winning. My eighth-grade gym teacher discovered that I was a natural runner with quick reflexes. That was when my brother Larry for the first time recognized me as a human being and began to take an interest in me. He worked on developing my stride so that it was longer and kept me low to the ground. Now, in high school, I'm a varsity runner.

"You have to ask yourself why you run," Jim said.

"I run because I love to compete. I want to win."

"That's not really why you run. You run to test yourself," he said.

"That's so crazy. I am basically a lazy person. I do it only to win."

"Look," he said, "I kill myself to learn the cello for the same reason. We have everything too easy."

"Come on, Jim. Don't lay this guilt trip on us."

He disintegrated *that* original thought with a stare. "We lead insulated lives. We don't feel life's bumps."

Jim is my oldest friend, but I've never understood this side of him. He's the conscience of the world; periodically he convinces himself that he's undeserving. And that I am too. When he's way down, there's no way to lift him. He has given up many luxuries—like nice clothes—and even some necessities. Recently he has begun to cut down on food as if he thinks that if he eats less the world will be a better place. He's given up lunches in school altogether.

"I like my insulation, Jim."

"It's not fair though, is it? We have so much."

"Maybe not. But it's not as if we did anything wrong either."

A wild look came into his eyes. "The thing is to do something right. The thing is to *do* something!"

"Sure. You're a gigantic almost-seventeen and I'm a big sixteen. What can we do? Not much. Some day we might do—spectacular things. You might win the Nobel Prize for music."

5

"Airhead. They don't give the Nobel Prize for music."

"All right. For peace then. I wouldn't be surprised. Meanwhile, let's enjoy what we've got."

"Music is its own prize," he said. "I love the cello."

We were at the corner where he turned off. "Can you carry this monster?" he asked, passing me the branch.

"Cross-country Carole?" I scoffed. "Woman athlete? No problem."

He took off. It was more a bough than a branch, and I was practically staggering under it by the time I got it home. Not because it was so heavy, but because I was suffering oxygen loss; my new Calvin Klein jeans presented a small problem in survival even when I wasn't carrying saplings. Comfort was a small price to pay for jeans that looked the way these did. Tighter than skintight. I was faced with a personal crisis. I would have to give up my daily Hershey bars—two a day—for a while, or these jeans would have to be put away. It was too terrible a decision to make, so I put it off, ate my chocolate, and suffered.

Mom and Dad were sitting in the living room giggling and whispering like idiots. Something was definitely up.

"Carole," Mother called. (I'm named for the great Lombard. Clark Gable is the only thing she and I have in common. She was married to him, and I adore him as Rhett Butler.) "Come in here, please."

"Coming in a sec." What could they be up to? They

must have bought something sensational. We're a shopping family. There had been Jacuzzi talk for months. I grabbed a fistful of stuffed celery. Mom keeps the refrigerator stocked for the ravaging hordes. That's me mostly since my brother Larry left to ravage Providence, Rhode Island. I do my best.

Into the living room I went armed with tree and celery stalks.

"Birnam Wood come to Dunsinane," Daddy said. He's a Shakespeare buff who seems to have memorized the complete works. But this time I recognized the line. We had to read *Macbeth* in school, and afterward Brutal Blake put the Birnam Wood bit up on his chalkboard as our quote of the week. The army, in the play, advances behind branches. Pretty dumb, I thought, to pretend a forest is walking even if a weird old witch did predict that it would. "Sometimes you have to suspend disbelief," Blake wrote on my essay paper. "You do it for *Star Wars* and *E.T.* Why not for Shakespeare?" He had a point.

My mouth was wonderfully full of celery and cream cheese and walnuts. I crunched away. "*Macbeth*," I said, identifying the quote.

Daddy smiled with pleasure at my knowledge. Mom murmured, "What lovely leaves!" I thought I'd lay it on a little and really jolt them both. "'A thing of beauty is a joy forever,'" I said, when I could speak.

That really did shock them. The two of them were constantly mourning the fact that all I ever memorized were rock lyrics. (I do know dozens of them. I hear a

7

good song once and it stays with me.) My parents spent a lot of time worrying about me and how ignorant I would grow up. So they absolutely went bananas over this quote. I was a little nervous that they might ask who said it and I'd have to say *Mrs. Monroe*, so I took a huge bite of my last celery stalk. My mouth was too full for talking. Next time I would be sure to ask the author's name. *Footnotes, footnotes, footnotes,* Blake constantly chanted. *Know your sources.*

"I didn't know you'd read Keats," Daddy began happily.

The new Ashland literary authority smiled modestly and desperately changed the subject. "Mom, would you buy low calorie cream cheese? I'm gaining weight."

"Sure," she said, "but I doubt it's the cream cheese."

"What else could it be?"

She was amused. "Let me take those leaves from you," she said, and I gave them over gladly, making a solemn silent vow to read Keats, nothing but Keats. She stood the branch in her pewter pitcher. It looked stunning; the leaves glowed. Our living room is really neat. Since Daddy had a busy and prosperous practice and Mom loves to shop and is houseproud—her word—the whole place is remarkably attractive and comfortable, but the living room is her particular pride. It is carpeted in chocolate brown and furnished with American colonial-style furniture. The pewter pitcher has four matching beer tankards, and there is also some old china and silver. Our andirons and fire tools are more than a hundred years old.

The branch beautifully in place, Mom sat back down and the two of them began to smile and then to giggle. Mind you, these were my parents acting like idiots.

I thought, they've bought some crazy antique, some candlesnuffer or butter churn. Either an antique or some ultra-modern high-tech household invention. Maybe some gismo that self-dusts or scents the air on command. Our garage was packed with gadgets that once looked sensational on display in Conran's and Macy's. Among the now-discarded items my parents once couldn't resist are a rowing machine, a corn popper, an exercise bicycle, a calculator, two electric vegetable choppers, a yogurt maker, a massager shower head, two cordless phones, a digital coffeemaker, a coffee bean grinder, five different gravy skimmers, a blender, a food processor, a pasta maker, two griddles, an ice crusher, and at least a dozen do-it-yourself repair kits that somehow never did-it-themselves.

Out here, mall-shopping is a favorite pastime. Most Saturdays go that way and everyone minds that there are Blue Laws that keep the stores shut on Sundays. We were all great shoppers in our family—Larry, too. I'm the one who was most conscious of labels. Sometimes the labels were the best part of the items I bought. Those designer creations can be pretty weird. Larry just bought preppy stuff. (Larry, by the way, is named for Laurence Olivier. If there had been a third child, he/she would have been named Groucho, I swear.)

"Sit down, Carole," Daddy said.

"Please, may I take ten minutes and go upstairs and change?"

"What'll you be when you're changed?" he asked. It was a very old routine we had.

"Comfortable," I said. "These new jeans look great but I haven't been able to breathe in them all day."

"Why didn't you buy your size?"

"They are her size," Mom said. "Too small is her size this year. Too small is everyone's size."

"Right down," I told them and I was off up the stairs.

First I put on my old stone-washed Levi's, which feel like gigantic pajamas (and look like them too) and my Springsteen T-shirt. I tried to solve my dilemma. Maybe if I cut down to one Hershey bar a day and increased my running time, I could lose weight. One bar! I couldn't just quit cold turkey. One bar distributed over the day.

While I was washing all the eye gook off—liner, mascara, and shadow is all we're into in my grade; bright lipstick is so-o-o crude—I began to wonder what Daddy was doing in the living room so early. What happened to his office hours? I finished in a rush.

"Charge!" I yelled, as I came tearing down the stairs. Another family joke. They liked literary quotes. In the comedy *Arsenic and Old Lace*, the nutty nephew who thinks he is Teddy Roosevelt yells "Charge!" as he runs up and down stairs. What if it is only one word? It's a literary quote. My parents claimed there was no mystery to why I remembered this particular quote. It was

10

my mantra, they said, my secret formula because I use my credit card so much.

"Charge!" First to the refrigerator for more celery and then I burst into the living room where they sat waiting for me.

"You'll have to get a new mantra," Daddy said, oddly.

CHAPTER 2

The two of them were sitting there looking very mysterious. I sat on the deacon's bench along the wall near them. The sharp oversized kitchen scissors lay before them on the coffee table. Something was definitely up and I hadn't a clue.

In my mind I frantically reviewed the last few days. I was innocent. Whoever had done something or not done something, it was definitely not me. Not I. Neither of us first person pronouns was guilty.

Parents are something else to deal with. I never know whom I'm going to get: the liberal, Queen Victoria's double, my best friend, or a preacher. To be fair, my folks are bearable. I have friends with *real* problem parents. Monique Shapiro, my best friend, has a mother who is terrific but flaky. And Jim Dunham has parents who are uptight. My parents are pretty relaxed; they don't pry too much and they don't censor. They leave me alone except when it comes to drinks, drugs, and sex. They figure sixteen is too young to make those decisions so I get a little direction from them. Like they paralyze me with rules and case histories.

"Okay," I said, before my first bite of celery, "here I am. Let's hear it. What did you buy? A hot tub?"

They looked at each other significantly.

"No such thing," Daddy said. "Listen, Carole, for a long time I haven't been happy in what I'm doing."

That whopped me. "What have you been doing?"

"You know. Dentistry."

"This is the first I ever heard that you weren't happy in it." I tried to finish my mouthful. Celery is not a conversational vegetable. Olives and gherkins are much better. Artichokes are the worst. Maybe that's how they got their name; they choke off all conversation.

"Well, you're pretty preoccupied with yourself and Jim and Monique," Daddy said.

No argument. He was right. Jim and Monique are the people I spend most of my time with, and the ones I confide in most, in person and on the phone. For one thing, in our family we are all pretty busy, me with school and track (a good runner is a daily runner), Dad with dentistry and the Ashland Players, our local community theater, Mom with homemaking (never to be put down as housekeeping) and the League of Women Voters, and Larry with school and football, and now, I bet, sex.

13

"Besides," he continued, "I couldn't come to terms with it myself. I've been a dentist for so long. I needed to decide if my unhappiness was real or imagined."

"Boy, you are complicated," I said.

He smiled. "You didn't think so?"

He was right. I didn't. He was always so reliable and predictable. I was eager to move the conversation along, to get on with it and then go upstairs and listen to my new Dire Straits album. I was a bit uncomfortable. Heart-to-hearts with my parents have never been my thing, especially when the problem is not mine.

"I've decided to fly after the bluebird of happiness! To have my rendezvous with destiny! To chase rainbows!" Daddy said as if he were really telling me something.

I looked him in the eye and quoted Brutal Blake. "You are making sounds, Dr. Warner, but you are not communicating."

"I am not going to be a dentist any more."

"Ever? You're kidding, Daddy."

"No," he said, and Mom, sitting there beside him, shook her curly brown head to emphasize his answer. Mom is a pretty woman, tall; in fact, she's five foot nine, four inches taller than Daddy, and she has large brown eyes and creamy skin. I take after her. I'm tall with very long legs, and I look a lot like her. Her feet are a reasonable size, but mine are huge. Her mother and her friends teased her about marrying a short man but Mom says she always thought Daddy was just the right height. He's certainly a lot better looking than

14

Henry Kissinger who also has a tall attractive wife. I admire Mom's independent mind. She decides things for herself.

Her face was bright with excitement. "Daddy's giving up his practice," she said, "except Sundays when possible."

"If I'm not on the road," he added mysteriously.

"On the road?" I was way out of synch. "You are going to be a traveling salesman? Just because you liked the way Dustin Hoffman played Willie Loman?"

Daddy shook his head. "I'm going to be a professional actor."

I went into shock. It was too hard for me to believe what I'd heard, so I slapped my thighs as I laughed. "Yeah, and I'm going to be Diana Ross. In fact, all the Supremes."

"It shouldn't be such a surprise," Mom said. "Your dad has always loved the theater. You know he reads everything on the subject. And he's been taking acting courses and studying it all his life."

"But that's amateur. A hobby."

"Exactly. And now I'm going to try to do it professionally."

"In the movies?"

No, it turned out. Not in the movies. On the stage. Hollywood acting, as far as he was concerned, was selling out. If he had to do things purely for money, he'd make TV commercials or whatever, but the New York stage was what he really was aiming for.

"What's this selling-out business?" I asked him. "Are

15

you saying Robert Redford, Paul Newman, Richard Gere have all sold out?"

"No. Each man decides for himself. I decide for me. The stage is what I want."

It was bizarre. Until this conversation I had no idea any of this was going around in his head. I really don't know when/if other families talk. I mean really *talk*. Our family doesn't see each other so much. At mealtime we mostly eat and run. Evenings in our lives are always busy times. Mom and Dad go out a lot. Either they're doing something with the Ashland Players or they're off somewhere watching a play, on Broadway, Off Broadway, Off Off Broadway. There is not a musty cellar in the northeastern U.S. with two or more rows of folding chairs that Dr. and Mrs. Albert Warren haven't been to. Yep, that's his name, Albert Warren. Carole Warren wouldn't be bad for the stage; Laurence Warren might be okay. But, Albert? Sounds just like a New Jersey dentist. Daddy said he didn't plan to change it. He thought it suited him. It had a certain strength of character.

I suppose I should have seen it coming, but I'm not very observant. I mean—plays have always been very much a part of our lives. When I was younger, we used to act out books—*Winnie the Pooh* and *Mutiny on the Bounty*—but it was for fun. Lots of people entertain themselves with hobbies, but they don't go around giving up their professions to be full-time stamp collectors or tennis players. Jim's father collects miniature soldiers and sets them up in various historical battle formations he gets from books; is he going to stop being a banker and play with his soldiers full time?

Don't get me wrong. I like plays. Sometimes my parents talk me into going to the theater with them. That's how come I was the only one in the Ashland Middle School to see Dickens's *Nicholas Nickleby,* which was positively incredible, three plays in one, condensed and acted on a single Sunday, a hundred dollars a ticket! But mostly I talk my way out of going with them because our tastes are so different. I like musicals, I like comedies, and if I must I can take a little Shakespeare—not walking forests, maybe, but *Romeo and Juliet* and *The Taming of the Shrew.* My parents go more for these experimental things with no props or all broken-down furniture in dim light. One play had a guy talking into a tape recorder and eating bananas. Another had these sad characters sitting around a dump talking. Depressing. Very bleak.

It is true that Daddy always loves to talk about his college days and the Thespian Society and the fun they had. How he once played Mark Antony wearing a bedsheet and the safety pin holding it opened so he gave the great funeral speech in his powder-blue boxer shorts. But that was ages ago.

"If you loved acting, why didn't you do it when you were young?" I asked him.

"—ger," Mom corrected me. "Younger."

"A good question. Nobody forced me into dentistry. Since my father was a dentist, I just naturally went into it. I was too dumb to recognize I had another calling."

17

"Calling?"

"Yes. Vocation. Something I *have* to do." He came over and sat down next to me and took my hand. "There are a lot of questions I don't know the answers to, but I do know that for almost twenty years I've done dentistry and I'm a good dentist, but my heart is not in it any more. Literally."

"You mean figuratively." Blake had worked on those terms with us: literally means truly; figuratively means symbolically.

Daddy shook his head. "Literally, Carole. I've been having chest pains. Nothing serious, but my blood pressure is up and Dr. Spencer thinks it's stress. He thinks it's because I'm doing what I don't want to do. You won't believe what he said to me. Don Spencer, who hasn't made a single joke in all the years I've been going to him, said, 'Albert, you are stuck in the root canal.'"

Pretty unbelievable for Dr. Spencer to make even that joke, but even more unbelievable for him to make that diagnosis. "But what about the pressure of running around trying to get acting jobs? It will probably kill you."

"Then that's the way I want to go. No drill in my hand. No water pick. Just a script. Footlights dimming and harps rippling in the background instead of the sound of a patient gagging."

"Daddy, be serious. We're having a serious talk."

"I've never been more serious. I've been thinking about this for years. It won't kill me. It will be

18

hard, but it's what I want to do more than anything else."

"What will happen to us? Where will we get money?"

He was smiling at me but the smile was a bit unsteady like his smiles when I fell off my bike or twisted my ankle in the county track meet. It was a smile only face-deep. "We've got some savings. And we just paid off the last of our mortgage. In a way that makes this possible. The roof over our heads is secure. And it's a nice roof, nicer than most people's."

I liked our roof fine; it kept off the rain and the snow and the wind. But he was not answering me. Then he did answer. "Your mother is going back to work."

"But she likes staying home." I turned to her, to the lady who could never understand why our prosperous women neighbors wanted to get up real early mornings and run into the city and work. As far as she was concerned, she'd said a million times, she had it made. Mrs. Antiquer, Mrs. Course-taker, Mrs. Suburbia. She was always busy, never bored.

"I do like staying home," she said, "and I could go on doing it. But it's your father's turn now to do what he's always wanted to do. I don't really mind. I used to be a crackerjack secretary. And that evening course in word-processing that I took last year will come in handy." At the time I'd thought it was crazy for her to take a course she didn't need. I mean, we don't own a word processor. But she said that she was intrigued by the wave of the future.

19

"Anyway," Mom finished up, "it's a challenge."

I made a lemon-sucking face. Sour. Challenge is a guidance-counselor word. Like share.

"Listen," Mom reminded me, "equal rights means equal for everyone. Even Daddy."

"Who will hire you after you've been home so many years? Will you make enough money to support us all?"

Mom was shaking her head. "There's going to be a lot less money around here. But someone will hire me. I do an honest day's work. Daddy and I don't know the answers to your questions. We're taking a big chance. But he needs to do it. Nobody should be forced to work at a job that doesn't give him satisfaction."

"He earns a good living. That must give him satisfaction."

"Not enough," Daddy said. "Too many people spend their lives doing things they're not crazy about because they have no other way of earning money. They're trapped. I want to see if I can get out of my trap."

I couldn't think of any more arguments. My eyes focused on that big scissors lying in front of us all. "What's the scissors for?"

"We're going to have a credit-card cutting ceremony," Mom said.

"Wha-at?"

"No more credit-card buying. For any of us."

"Mom—I can't. I don't carry cash around like you and Dad. I can't write checks. I can't manage."

"Carole," Daddy said, reaching for his own wallet, "get your card."

Mom was headed for the drawer in the sideboard where she stores her purse.

He actually cut his cards. He had five. Then Mom cut hers. There were small piles of plastic shards on the coffee table.

"Carole—" Mom said.

I didn't move.

"People lived a long time without these," Daddy said. "Go get yours." He looked at me steadily. "Carole?"

What could I do?

I went.

CHAPTER 3

It really killed me to go up those stairs and take that card out of my wallet. Once I cut it I would be cutting off Saturdays at the mall. Gone would be Sam Goody and The Gap and The Hunan Palace and all the department stores. I would be cutting off a whole way of life that I loved.

The condemned woman inched down the stairs. I was crying. I can't believe now that I was crying so much then, but I really was. I could hardly see.

"Go ahead." Daddy handed me the scissors. "Cut it. We'll send the pieces back and close the accounts."

I cut it.

"You're not really crying for your credit card," Daddy said.

"No. I'm scared."

"About not having a credit card in your wallet?"

"About everything, Daddy. You. This whole business."

"Sorry, sweetie. You'll get used to it. This is a family of four smart, able-bodied, resourceful people. Surely we'll find ways to manage."

Four! It hit me. Larry safe at Brown in Providence. Or Larry thinking himself safe. What about him? Did he know? Would he have to leave Brown? He loved it there. "What about Larry?" I asked.

"I wrote to him, so by now he knows," Daddy said. "He'll have to get a part-time job, and apply for student loans next year."

"He'll be freaked by this." I was sure of it. Larry beat me at spending. That's not hard when you buy all your major clothing at J. Press. "He's enjoying college so much."

"He'll continue to enjoy himself," Mom said. "He'll just have to help pay for it."

"As you will, Carole," Daddy said. "There won't be money around here for a while for clothes and going out a lot. Unless, of course, I'm *discovered* right away."

"Couldn't you wait till I finish high school? Just two more years."

"No," Daddy said quietly. "After high school there'll be college and then maybe graduate school. I'm forty-two, which is late enough to start an acting career. Any later and I'll only be good for senior citizen parts."

I'm ashamed of what came out of my mouth next. My only excuse is that I was so upset I didn't really know what I was saying. "No one will hire you," I said, getting up. "Who's going to hire a short New Jersey dentist as an actor?"

"Carole," Mom said, and her voice was gritty, "have we ever said anything like that to you? Even once? When you wanted ballet lessons even though you were a foot taller than the others? And baton twirling? And ice skating? And guitar? Did we ever step on your dreams?"

"But I'm sixteen. He's forty-two." I really did not think I was wrong. But I felt oddly ashamed of what I was saying. "He has responsibilities. He's a father and a husband."

"He's not ducking those responsibilities," Mom said. "Between us we will take care of you and Larry. There just won't be a lot of money around to squander."

"You guys taught us how to live that way."

"I know," Daddy said grimly. "I'm afraid now we all have other lessons to learn. Me, too."

"I'd like to be excused," I said, and I left the two of them sitting there. What did they expect? That I'd yell "Whoopee!" at their dumb news? Maybe they really thought I was a different kind of kid. But I'm what they raised in the 1980s. Credit-Card Carole.

I went into my room and lay down on the bed. I was petrified. Ever since I could remember, Daddy had spent five days a week in the clean bright room attached to our house working on patients' teeth. A lot of things happened in the world: the giant elm tree outside my window died and had to be chopped down; I developed breasts at last; Larry graduated from high school and went away to college; I started running, seriously. Other things changed, but Daddy's office hours were a constant.

I comforted myself. Larry would call home. Or maybe he would come home and talk sense to them. They listened to him sometimes. They figured a person in college was capable of reasoning. For them, sixteen was still infancy. And at that moment, I felt as helpless as an infant.

I felt awful about what I had said to Daddy. He really is a wonderful actor. When he played Stage Manager in *Our Town* he was so good, I swear I forgot he was my father. But he was too old to start his career now. No one would hire him for a real part and pay him money to act.

The phone rang. I got it on the second ring. Larry!

As soon as I answered I could tell that something was different. The operator didn't say Niccolò Machiavelli or Dante Alighieri was calling anyone at this number, collect. (Larry is taking Italian history. Last term he was into German and we got weird late-night collect calls from Johann Wolfgang von Goethe or some creep named Metternich.) Anyway, Larry was paying for this call. It was a serious call.

"Hey, sibling," he said. "How's it going?"

"Backwards. Did you get their letter?"

"Yeah. Surprise, eh, Carole? You going to like having Frank Langella for a father?"

"Frank Langella?" I laughed bitterly. "It's more like Mickey Rooney."

"Hey, that's not nice."

"I don't feel like being nice. I think it's a crazy idea."

Silence on the wire. When Larry spoke again it was very softly as if he was afraid of being overheard. "Listen, Carole. Go with it. Dr. Spencer thinks Albert's got to do it. So, Albert's got to do it." Then his voice got louder. "It might even be interesting. We need to be shook up a little."

"But, Larry," I whispered into the phone, "we had to cut up our credit cards. There's not going to be any money around for anything. No one will pay him to act."

"Don't cry doom so fast. Mom is going back to work and she's good. You've seen her in action for the League of Women Voters. When she gets going she's amazing. And he's wonderful on the stage. In all those local productions, you thought he was sensational. When he did Bogie in *Play It Again, Sam*, we thought his imitation was incredible. Remember? He *was* Bogie. The best."

"He was very good, but those were amateur productions."

"You've got to give him a chance, kid. That's all he's asking for, a chance. He's not hocking the dental equipment. He's just giving it a rest."

"Larry, what will you do for money?"

Long pause. "Who knows? This year is paid for. I'll have to look into loans, I guess, later on. You know I was taking a bartending course here for laughs? Well, today I lucked into a bartending job for Saturday night. Sixty bucks plus overtime plus tips and all I can eat and drink. I think I'll find ways of picking up loot. It's kind of a challenge."

"Watch your language," I said. "It's kind of a drag."

I heard the downstairs door open. My parents were coming in. "Listen, let me tell them you're on the phone."

"Swing with it, Carole."

I called downstairs and told them. Daddy got on and Mom came upstairs and picked up the extension.

"Sir Larry?" Daddy talking. "How's the boy?"

Whatever Larry said made him laugh and laugh. Mom stood there listening and grinning and looking very proud. You'd think they'd sent their only son to Brown to learn how to tend bar.

Daddy began to outline his strategy. "Starting Monday I'll answer open casting calls. All I need is to get into one show and then I get my Equity card and I'm launched. Yeah, that's all there is to it. Well, there aren't so many open casting calls, but they happen. I'll just have to look sharp."

Then it was Mom's turn. Her conversation was even weirder than Daddy's. "I'm trying to decide what to wear to look for work in," she said very seriously. "I'm

27

tending toward a tailored suit, but I don't want to look too masculine."

Larry's voice crackled at the other end, and she was delighted. "I couldn't, eh? You're good for my ego, son." She grew serious for a moment. "Larry, you understand that we *have* to do this."

She listened as he talked and she looked thoughtful. I must admit that my brother had surprised me. He'd always had whatever he wanted, and he was more than a bit of a snob. That's how come it was Brown University instead of Ohio State, which is Daddy's alma mater. It had to be IVY for Larry. It *had* to be. He sweated out that college-application time really suffering. And he never noticed money. He spent freely.

It hasn't quite hit him yet, I thought. He's looking at it like a game, something temporary that will soon be over. Wait till it hits him.

Mom was saying, "Yes, I know, it is. Terrifying and exciting. We feel as if we're starting over, son. And we're very optimistic." Then I heard Daddy, downstairs. "That is one thing an unemployed actor has to be. Eternally optimistic."

I left the hall and went into my room feeling thoroughly zonked. That is the one way a sixteen-year-old who has just had her credit card cut has to feel. Eternally pessimistic.

I was, in fact, desperate.

CHAPTER 4

I told my best friend, Monique Shapiro, next day at lunch. We were dining sumptuously in the school cafeteria on macaroni casseroles that tasted as if the macaroni had been liberally sprinkled with Tide instead of Parmesan cheese. I bet if a drop of water was spilled on my casserole I'd get soapsuds. Eating school junk had always been easier than carrying lunch from home. This was to be my last bought lunch and it was appropriately awful.

"I can't deal with my parents," I finished.

"Your trouble is you thought your parents were fixed in orbit forever, like the planets," she said. "If you had a mother like mine, there would be no problem."

Monique has *some* mother. She named Monique that way because she thought the French first name would make Shapiro sound exotic. She's another eternal optimist.

Maybe because of her bizarre name, Monique is tough. She's a redhead, good-natured but sometimes hard to read. She's got very pale white skin and green eyes. And though she's as tall as I am, her feet are nowhere near my blockbusters. Boys think she's a knockout. She goes her own way.

"My mother is a floater," Monique went on. "She floats through jobs and professions. She floats through religions. She floats through boyfriends. Nothing is anchored in her life except me. She looks after me and she loves me; otherwise, we give each other space."

"Don't you ever mind?"

"Sometimes, but not much. I'd rather have her than a robot parent. Do this, do that, and do it because *I* tell you to."

I thought about it. Ms. Shapiro was a dynamo. She was into a million things. She had read up on Zen and Yoga and aerobics, and she even liked contemporary music. Nobody's parents besides her liked rock. I mean nobody's parents. She changed sometimes right before my eyes. She was a redhead like Monique, but she owned different wigs, blond, auburn, jet black, and she had contact lenses to match. She also had the most incredible sense of style and color. She was never gaudy; she was dramatic but with taste. I admired her enormously. She was chic. Gloria—she insisted that Monique and her friends call her Gloria—had a lively sarcastic manner. She ran her own interior decorating business from her house so she was in and out a lot. Mr. Shapiro had disappeared when Monique was five. Gloria had kept herself and Monique going by hard work, talent, and ingenuity. She was the biggest advocate of women-learning-how-to-take-care-of-themselves that I knew.

"My father was an alcoholic," Monique told me, matter-of-factly.

"How do you know?"

"Gloria said so. He was the nicest man alive when he was sober, smart and funny. And very handsome. But he drank. From the very beginning, she knew that about him."

"Why did she marry him?"

"She was going to save him. She was going to be the good woman who would keep him from wasting his life."

I was always startled by the straightforward way Monique and her mother talked about things. My folks try to be direct, but many topics embarrass them and then they operate like the CIA. Gloria will give you a straight answer to anything if she can.

She's really a smart woman—except about men. Monique says mostly she keeps falling for the same kind of guy. I've been over at their house several times when one of her boyfriends came by to pick her up. Glitzy. Monique is right; they're all glitzy.

The bell rings and in comes a handsome guy, a smooth dresser—designer clothes, big rings on his fingers, gold neckchains, too much aftershave lotion—and he's parked his fancy car outside.

Monique says none of them are ever as smart as her mother. Each one hangs around a while and gives Gloria a big rush. They laugh together a lot at first. Then, either she gets tired of him and dumps him, or he disappears. She gives up on men for a little while until she finds another or he finds her.

"We were getting along just great," Monique said now, "except that this morning just before I left she said she thinks she's had it with the Jogger."

"Oh, no." I was really sorry. For a while it looked as if Gloria had broken her wrong-man pattern with this nice, tall, not-so-handsome guy—his hair was thinning—with a great smile. His name was Harold. Gloria hated the name so she nicknamed him "Jogger" because that was what he did every morning. She liked him a lot, enough so she went out and bought a neat bunch of sweatpants and tops, and she even bought some for Monique. The three of them would go running together some mornings. Monique loved it and Gloria seemed to be having fun.

"What's the Jogger done to make her mad?" I asked.

Monique was really unhappy. "He truly cares about her, so he's been after her to quit smoking. He says it's killing her breathing, so she can't really run—and, eventually, it will kill her and damage me."

"Gee, that's no reason to dump him."

"Gloria doesn't appreciate advice from anyone. She says he's nagging."

"You should tell him to hold off, take it easy."

"I did," Monique said, "but he won't listen. He thanked me, and he said he couldn't have a relationship that wasn't honest. He likes Gloria too much to keep quiet when she's doing something dumb."

"Monique, don't you have the feeling that grownups are irrational? I mean, we expect them to be grown up and they're not. They're not what we expect at all."

"Especially my mother."

"Not especially. Look at what my father is doing."

"I think that's neat," she said. "I hope I can come and see him in a play."

That goes to show about friends, even close friends. I understood her perfectly about her mother, but she didn't understand me and my feelings at all.

"I have to carry lunch from now on," I said. "Goodbye to all these cafeteria banquets. I'll really miss them."

Monique loved the idea. "I'll join you. I can use the money better. We can pack lunches alternate days and we won't tell what we're bringing. It will be a surprise."

"What a nifty idea. Being poor may turn out okay yet. Who brings first?"

"Let's toss," Monique suggested. "Loser brings first."

It was me. Pepperoni and cream cheese on bagels, I decided. We are both lifetime pepperoni freaks.

CHAPTER 5

Saturday was when it really hit me. It was a sunny gorgeous Saturday, which made it even worse. You have to understand that Saturday in our part of the world is mall day. Pizzas or burritos or cheeseburgers day. Resting-your-feet-at-a-movie-in-the-Tenplex-after-hours-of-shopping day. Paradise Day. Buying and selling, our patriotic-duty day. That's the way the American economy keeps rolling.

I was accustomed to getting up early on Saturdays, about eight-thirty or so; then I could be at the mall by ten-thirty. It's nice to be there first before the crowd picks over all the new styles. At that hour the stores and dressing rooms are pretty empty and I got to try on anything I wanted to. Some stores like to look busy so the salespeople don't ask questions. Once I spent a whole hour trying on wedding gowns and it was almost noon before the clerk came into the dressing room and said, "Planning to be a child bride?" She was very nice about it. People are in a better mood when they're not tired and hurried, so mornings are the best time at the mall. I thanked her for letting me try on so many gowns. "Come back in ten years," she said. Ten? Five. More likely three. The white silk gown with four tiers and seed pearls rimming each tier was a knockout. It was a classic. Three, five, even ten years in the future this would be *the* gown. The full skirt hid my big feet.

I've always enjoyed being the first to try on the latest clothes. I respect them; I take the pins and the tissue paper out carefully, and I unbutton all the buttons or unzip the zippers all the way. I liked to experiment with all kinds of combinations: slacks, jeans, skirts with sweaters and blouses or vests or jackets, layers of colors and mixes of stripes and solids. I'm a sucker for scarves and nice belts.

When I saw something I really liked a lot, when the whole outfit clicked and I could see myself in it on the pages of *Seventeen*, then I bought it. Sometimes I had to bring it back the next Saturday, if Mom thought it was too odd or too old for me or I'd overspent. She set the limit. But mostly I got to keep the really neat things I bought.

No more. I woke up early as usual but I wasn't going

anywhere. I had told Jean and Christa, the two kids I mainly shop with, that I was tremendously busy this Saturday at home, and that was why I couldn't come shopping. They were pretty surprised since I am usually lead shopper. I would rather go shopping with Monique, but she hates shopping. Probably, she says, because her mother loves it so and used to drag her along. Jean and Christa have MasterCards and Christa has Visa. They live in Old Ashland which means huge houses and enormous plots of land around them. We are really only shopping friends. We love to spend our Saturdays the same way, but otherwise we aren't close. I wouldn't admit this to anyone else, but my private opinion of them is not so high. I would never confide in them because they tell what other people have told them confidentially, and they laugh and make fun of their friends behind their backs. In fact, they make fun of anyone they think of—like Angie, who is black and is my cross-country partner. I know Angie is smart, and I certainly know she's a fantastic runner. They don't even really know her, but they think her fuzzy hair is weird.

"That's her natural hair," I told them.

"She could straighten it if she wanted to look normal," Christa said. "The others do." She meant the other four black kids in our school.

"Straight hair is *not* normal for her. You mean normal like us."

"The majority decides what's normal," Jean said, ever-loyal to Christa.

36

"No," I said. "Normal is different for different people."

They both looked at me funny, and I didn't know how to argue my point but I still thought I was right. "Let's go look at denim jackets," I suggested, and we did. That conversation bothered me a lot. Why shouldn't Angie keep her hair the way she wanted? Their position was stupid. At least they didn't talk about her in front of me anymore.

Well, that part of my life seemed to be over forever. What would I tell Christa and Jean next Saturday? How long could I pretend? They would find out about Daddy anyway. Soon enough they would know he was only a Sunday dentist, and I didn't have enough money to come shopping Saturdays. But I didn't think that I could bring myself to tell them. Let them find out from someone else. They would. They were on the main gossip line. Let them laugh off by themselves.

So I moped around, cleaning up my room minimally. I picked the clothes up off the floor and shoved them into the closet and various drawers. The cleaning woman, who came once a week to straighten up and vacuum, had been dispensed with. Mom said we could easily do for ourselves. I suppose we can. I can't *easily*. Certainly not happily. Cleaning is the most unproductive menial job in the universe. You dust, and while you're dusting new dust is accumulating.

We split the chores. Democracy—everyone got to help. Guess what lucky person got to do the laundry? The laundry! Instead of Shopping Saturday I got Sudsing Saturday. I had to change all the towels (three and one dish towel), and all the bed linen (two beds equals four sheets and three pillowcases), and gather the dirty stuff up out of the hamper and put it in the washer and then the dryer. Meanwhile, I had to make up the beds and put out fresh towels. When the laundry was dry I had to fold it neatly and put it away.

"That's at least the whole morning," I grumbled to Mom.

"If you lived in India you'd be standing in a stream, waist-deep, pounding the clothes clean with a stone. Be grateful."

One thing about adults: no place is too far for them to wander in their heads when they're telling you how good you've got it and how much others are suffering. Wait till scientists explore more of outer space and find life out there; that generation of kids is going to hear about the Martians or the Plutonians or some other creatures and how tough they have it washing clothes with their bare tentacles.

"Using a stone sounds like fun," I said. "That's the way good jeans are washed. Stone-washed."

"It only *sounds* like fun. Don't fuss over a small chore like laundry."

"It doesn't seem like a small chore to me."

Mom frowned. "I suppose it's not your fault. It's my fault—our fault. You are terribly spoiled."

I hate that word spoiled. It makes me feel like a rotten banana. "Spoiled for what?"

"Real life. Most people in this world work hard. Many start working much younger than you are now."

"I'm only sixteen."

"I know how old you are, Carole. I'm your mother. Kids get responsibilities much earlier than at sixteen. But Daddy and I tried to make life as easy and pleasant as possible for you and Larry because we love you so much. It seems to have been a mistake."

"No," I said. "It was no mistake. It was just a big holiday. I'm sure I can learn to do whatever I have to do. But that doesn't mean I'll like it. This would be a better world if nobody had to do drone work. No pounding with stones and no doing any wash at all. Robots, that's the answer."

At least I had Mom smiling again.

Daddy got himself listed on the County Dental Exchange. On Friday—if he was going to be available the following Sunday—he would notify the exchange and they would refer patients to him. He and Mom made a million calls to patients directing them to other dentists. Of course he told everyone why and many of the patients asked if they could come see him on the stage. He was pleased.

Mom was suddenly a dynamo getting clothes ready for the whole week, buying food for quick meals, trying to be completely prepared. She didn't expect to be at home much. She hoped. The two of them were so incredibly energetic and optimistic it got to me. They were like two little kids before some big outing, some

giant picnic or circus. Like kids, they were sure everything would proceed as planned. To be told something's
going to happen, when you're a kid, is a guarantee.
What if it didn't? What if it rained on their picnic?
What if the circus didn't show?

I was scared.

So I folded the laundry as well as any robot might.
Capable Carole, that's me. Only—robots can't worry.
But I could. And I did.

CHAPTER 6

Jim and I were going to the movies together that night.

Jim is a year ahead of me in school, smart, studious, and a loner—like Monique. Each of my two closest friends has no other friend except me. Does that make me a loner too? It makes me lucky because they're the best. Who cares for crowds?

Jim has a seesaw personality, up and down. When he's up, he's hyper. Brilliant. When he's down, he's bleak. Those times I do my best to boost him. Otherwise, he's practically normal; that means he isn't a klutzy jock, he doesn't do drugs, and he's not a wimp. One remarkable thing about him: he's ambidextrous; both arms are equally strong and skilled at doing things: writing, throwing a ball, playing a cello.

We're just friends. We're not in love. We tell each

other what we think. We don't make out a lot. Just a little. Though Christa and Jean don't believe that. They have such fixed minds they can't imagine a *friendship* between a boy and a girl.

My friendship with Jim goes back to playground days when Rhonda, his family maid, would bring him there and Mom would bring me. (His mother has always been sickly, so Rhonda practically raised him.) Since I've always been big for my age—tall—I was just right opposite him on the seesaw. Once started we could go on and on without the grownups' help. That promoted the relationship.

In Ashland, the movies are the only entertainment within walking distance. Restaurants, discos, all the bright lights are in the other towns or along the highways. New Jersey law sets seventeen as the minimum age for drivers, so we're locked in. Weekends are long; it doesn't really matter what movie is showing, we often go. Going to the movies gets you out of your house. That's the main reason Jim goes. He dislikes his house. "The Dunham Depository and Private Museum," he calls it. "Between my mother's porcelain collection and my dad's miniatures, we've got a bigger exhibition than the Smithsonian. There should be a turnstile in our foyer and an admission charge. If they had dinosaurs it would be worth it, or if they cared about science or history or art. But soldiers and dishes? Expensive junk—in a world where children are starving."

"But your father earns his money. He doesn't take it away from those hungry children."

"Not directly. But my father is an investment banker. A lot of our money comes right out of South Africa."

I've thought about this for hours and hours—I couldn't be Jim's friend and not think about it—and I haven't come up with any answers. When you're sixteen years old and you don't like the way your father earns his money, there's not much you can do about it. Most kids wouldn't notice as long as the money's there, the more the better. I've tried all sorts of arguments on Jim. He knows he's stuck till he grows up and can earn his own living, but it gnaws at him. It's not that he hates his father. His father is kind if a bit distant and stuffy. Lots of kids have much worse fathers. To Jim, his father has become a symbol of injustice. And his mother is just the echo of his father.

"Be patient," is what I always end up advising him. "Run in place till you're old enough to take off. Then you'll go along your own course."

He would be patient, I think, if he could. He needs help because he can't.

When Jim came by, Daddy must have let him in. I was showering and didn't hear the doorbell. The first I knew he was here was when I emerged from the bathroom and was passing through the upper hall. I heard Daddy's voice, loud, down below. I was about to interrupt, to call down that I'd be there in a sec but I stayed quiet. Daddy had Jim cornered in the chair by the coat closet, the chair where people sit to pull their boots off and on. Daddy was orating. Jim was listening.

You all did love him once, not without cause:
What cause withholds you then to mourn for him?
Oh judgement! thou are fled to brutish beasts,
And men have lost their reason. Bear with me;
My heart is in the coffin there with Caesar,
And I must pause till it come back to me.

"Are the Ashland Players doing *Julius Caesar*, Dr. Warren?" Jim asked, surprised. He knew that classical plays never attracted much of an audience. Musicals and comedies brought in the crowds.

"No," Daddy said. "I was just remembering the lines."

"From when?"

"Twenty years ago."

Jim was impressed. "Wow. You're a wonderful actor, Dr. Warren. You could probably have been on Broadway."

"Tell that to Carole, Jim. She has her doubts."

That must have confused Jim because he knew I thought Daddy was sensational in the local productions.

"She'll explain it all to you," Daddy said. He came to the foot of the stairs and called for me to come down. I was already on my way.

"That part should be played in powder-blue boxer shorts," I said, and Daddy laughed. Jim just looked bewildered. I hurried him outside. "We're high on unemployment," I said, once the door was closed. "You won't believe this, Jim, but Dr. Albert Warren has come unstrung." As we walked, I explained about the lost toga in the college play and then I told Jim the news.

"You mean he's giving it up? He's not going to work on teeth any more?"

"So he says. He'll be a Sunday dentist for his friends and a few old patients. He'll take some emergency cases. But not full time."

"I never heard anything like it. It's remarkable. He's finding his own destiny."

"Looking for it," I conceded.

"Wait till I tell my folks."

He was really enthusiastic. I squeezed his arm, and at first I didn't say anything. I was thinking about his parents. They're totally conservative. They think the Social Security system is dangerous socialism. They believe that poor people are poor because they want to be, and anyone who takes government help or food stamps is lazy. His father does good works; he sits on many charity committees and museum boards. We read about him all the time in our local newspapers. So he isn't heartless or cruel like Ralph Nickleby in Dickens's book, but he is sort of far away from real everyday life. Jim's views are all exactly opposite to his. His father says Jim is a refugee from the sixties—an out-of-season flower child—and Jim says that's a compliment. He says the Vietnam War was a bad war. His father says there never was a good war, but that one was necessary. They go round and round like that. Both his parents would have loved to send him to a prep school—so he'd be prepped for the good life—but he refused to go.

Suddenly, I was scared. A dentist's daughter had

been an acceptable friend for Jim as far as his parents were concerned. Now, Mr. Dunham might decide that I was the wrong kind, a bad influence. "Don't tell your father about my father, Jim. Please. He won't understand and it will only make him dislike me."

"He doesn't like you too much anyway. Nothing personal, you understand. How could it be? He doesn't know you. He's never liked anyone I liked. I must not permit minor distractions to interfere with my real life's goals, he says."

"What are they?"

"To 'make my way.' 'Making my way' means 'making money.'"

"Is that really the way he talks to you?"

"Sure. That's the way my father talks to everyone," Jim grinned. "I think he probably wore charcoal gray diapers and a two-button Carter's baby vest with thin lapels. You think a tie, too?"

"Come on. He can't be so straight. After all, he does have those miniature soldiers. That's unusual."

"That's just a hobby. A very expensive one, too. Those miniatures cost. Many bankers have hobbies—golf, or stamps, or collecting some weird thing. Hobbies are acceptable. What's not acceptable is doing anything unpredictable, anything on the spur of the moment. That is *verboten*."

"It sounds like a safe life."

"Safe and selfish," he agreed. "Pretend that there's nobody hungry out there. Contribute to charity, but be sure it's deductible."

46

"You're hard on him, Jim."

"He's hard on me." A wild gleam lit his gray eyes.

"What about your mother?"

"She's like wax—soft, pliable. It's not her fault. I can't ever remember her being healthy." When he talked about his mother, his face softened. "She has no energy. When you're sick, nothing else counts but just getting through the day. Whatever else is happening seems at a great distance. That's what I've learned from my mother." He was lost in his own thoughts for a while, and then he came back to the subject of his father. "But I'm tough and he's beginning to recognize that now. He wanted me to take French as my second language, but I said I wanted Chinese. Guess what? Or, rather, guess who's taking Chinese next term? He hates it, but I'm taking Chinese."

"Why Chinese?"

His lean, intense face cracked a grin. "Because it's the language of a Communist country, and that drives my father wild."

"Why not Russian? It's probably easier."

"He's afraid of the 'Yellow Peril'. He thinks Asiatics are going to take over the whole world, the way the Japanese and Koreans have taken over the electronics market. Actually, I'd love to be able to speak and read Chinese, but that's secondary."

"I wish I had a safe life."

"Come on. You don't wish your father was a banker." Jim put his arm around my shoulders and we walked

47

close together in step. "You wouldn't wish that in a million years."

"Well, I'm scared."

"Of what? Things will be different for a while, that's all. Nothing will ever be different in my life."

"One thing might. You might not want to hang out with me so much. I'm lower class."

He laughed. "Oh, I like being with celebrities. You think your father will give me an autographed picture?"

"I can arrange it for a fee. I have to figure out some way to make money."

"Wait." He stopped walking. "Don't get mad. I've got an idea."

"Why should I get mad?"

"My mother was talking this morning about calling the high school employment office. Since Rhonda just cooks and serves now and does very light work, the idea is for a female student to come in twice a week to dust and vacuum upstairs. The heavy work is done by our cleaning service. Mostly the job would be to dust the porcelains and Dad's miniatures."

"No! I'm not mad at you, but absolutely not! I hate housework, and what I hate most of all is dusting."

"Too bad. Five dollars an hour is what she's going to offer because the breakables have to be handled carefully. Rhonda figures about four hours a week would do it. And I could talk them into hiring you."

I squeezed his arm in gratitude. Whatever my father ended up doing for a living—and whatever I had to do, or Mom, or Larry—it didn't matter in the slightest to

Jim. Growing up in that snobby, wealthy house had made him aware of what was snobby and wealthy. Aware of it and wary of it. He was my friend.

Larry phoned us on Sunday at noon. He had earned eighty dollars including tips, as a bartender, and he'd had a marvelous time. There was this blond in red sequins who had a thing for bartenders. He couldn't tell me more because Parental Guidance was suggested. I told him it was all a hallucination.

The whole tone of the call was up, up, and away. If he had any fears or doubts or objections, no one was going to hear them. I have to admit that I was beginning to realize that my brother was a nicer person than I'd thought.

Good luck, he wished everyone. He talked fast, faster than I had ever heard him talk, because he was paying for the phone call! Good luck to me in whatever part-time job I found. Good luck to Mom who would be job hunting in big offices. To Daddy, of course, he didn't just say good luck. He said, "I know it's premature, but break a leg!"

CHAPTER 7

I've got some news that would surprise Mr. Darwin.

Evolution took a wrong turn; humans were not ready to be bipeds. They should have stayed quadrupeds. I learned that from my parents' first days of job hunting. Two feet were simply not enough. The most vulnerable parts of my mother and father were their feet. They'd start out in the morning looking terrific and feeling great and they'd crawl home in the evening. Showers and dinner and then a rest afterward revived them. All except their feet.

Mom set out each morning in a tailored suit, white soft blouse, black high heels. It was her serious outfit, the one she wore to school board meetings and other official functions, her Mrs. Citizen disguise. In it she was a *presence*. It now doubled fine for Mrs. Efficiency.

"Man-tailored clothes," she said to me, "because it's a man-tailored world."

"You really think it matters? You think they hire that way?"

"I'm afraid it's an important factor, kiddo. Someday it will be different."

"To hire by clothes is *so* dumb."

"True. But we don't make the rules."

Those early mornings were a strange time. Mom kissed me and Daddy good-bye and then she was gone. Ten minutes later, Daddy, looking his best, left to catch a bus to the city. I felt odd being the last one home in an empty house on a school morning. I took my book-bag and I locked up, but I was so unused to the stillness that I felt uneasy and I came back to check the door locks after I'd walked away. Of course, they were locked. Once I even went all the way back inside to make sure the stove was off and then realized that it had not been turned on—we'd all had yogurt for breakfast. There is something very safe in knowing that your parents are around all the time. Usually both of mine were there or right nearby, so this was totally new.

As I walked to school, I thought about latchkey children, young kids of working parents left alone all day, doorkeys around their necks. We had read about them in social studies and seen a documentary. But I hadn't grasped what it must be like to be seven, eight, or nine, and completely on your own. It's scary.

What ifs? began to occur to me. Scenes of devastation and death flashed into my mind: bus accidents, explosions in the Lincoln Tunnel, fires, floods, earthquakes. All because of an empty house. When was the last time there was an earthquake on the eastern seaboard? I had to force myself to stop thinking that frantic way. My parents were adults. Smart. Competent. They could take care of themselves.

During the school day (especially during lunch, which continued to be superior, Monique and I vying to do *great* sandwiches) I comforted Monique, who was tremendously sad about the situation with the Jogger. He was still coming around, but things at her house were really bad. The Jogger had talked Gloria into a trial nonsmoking period. She was not grateful. In fact, she was a wreck, tense, angry, and resentful of everyone and everything. "She's hooked," Monique kept saying. "Always before when she wanted to stop something—eating sweets, drinking too much coffee, overspending, anything—she just made up her mind, and she did it. She believed it was possible. That's why she believed my father could stop drinking. And now *she can't* stop smoking. She can't!"

"She stopped," I pointed out.

"She can't live this way. She'll go back."

"Maybe not. You always say she's so strong."

"Gloria is strong, Carole, but smoking is an addiction, I swear. Her hands go reaching out for the pack, automatically. Even when there is none. Before she opens her eyes in the morning."

Together, that afternoon, we made our second secret vow. Our first, sworn the year before, was No Sex Until

52

We Are Married. We had considered the problem endlessly; we read a lot of Judy Blume and Norma Klein and we reviewed biology books. And then we decided for ourselves. Let other people do whatever they want to. For Monique and me, holding off was what we chose to do.

And now we decided that we would never smoke or use any drug. Never! Not because we were such good kids, such saints. Because we were terrified of getting hooked. It made sense; if you're a teen, waiting and dreaming of the time you'll be independent and on your own, you don't want to tie up with anything that will hobble that independence.

I like making myself a promise and including Monique as witness. It's very hard to keep a pledge I make only to myself. I've been trying to fight the chocolate war alone for a very long time. When the pressure builds or I get tempted or a little curious, I need reinforcement. If I have to face my friend, that helps stop me. Monique is just the same.

I did my best to cheer her up about Gloria, but I knew things looked really bad. Juveniles can't do much about adult delinquents. We're just stuck with them.

My parents' hopes were so high that first week, I got caught up in the adventure of it too; new territories, new people, new possibilities. Daddy had the whole thing plotted out very carefully. No half-hearted amateur try; this was to be a campaign waged by a professional. He'd researched it thoroughly and he knew what it required.

In the closet of his office were five hundred copies of his resumé printed on the back of his composites, eight-by-ten sheets with two pictures of him on them: one a "straight" picture showing him exactly as he is with a pleasant smile on his face; the other, in trenchcoat, with makeup and stubbly beard, as Bogie in *Play It Again, Sam*. In his back-up portfolio, he had pictures of himself in costume in dozens of roles. Just let someone ask. He was about as ready as he could be. He began papering theatrical agencies, companies, showcases, and dinner theaters with his materials.

Meanwhile, Mom was being interviewed all over New Jersey. "Overqualified and underexperienced," seemed to be the catchphrase of the time. Overqualified meant she was smart and educated and skilled; underexperienced meant, of course, that she hadn't worked during the last twenty years. The punishment for not working was low salary offers for idiot jobs.

At night we sat and talked together more than we had ever before. Mostly the tube stayed dark. There was so much to tell. Daddy ran across Jack Lemmon in a men's room. Marlo Thomas lent him a pen in an agency. Cleavon Little offered him a stick of gum.

"Did you save it?" I asked.

"No. I chewed it."

"Daddy! It was a souvenir."

"What would he have thought if I'd pocketed his gum?"

I could see that it would have looked weird.

"What kind of gum?"

"Trident Cinnamon."

"Yuk! Cleavon Little chews that?"

"What did you think he chews?"

"Hubba Bubba at least."

We sat around and talked. I did my homework and they rested their feet. Each night we went to sleep on possibilities.

Friday night Daddy came home early with little to report. He and I were in the kitchen whipping up a one-dish dinner, keema, an Indian curry you do with chopped meat, onions, spices, and a vegetable. You put it all on rice. *Voilà*. Dinner! I was slicing the cabbage while he fried the onions and spices and meat. Just as I dumped the cabbage into the skillet, we heard the front door open and a happy voice break into "La Marseillaise." Triumph and victory!

In walked Mom on tired feet, white flat bakery box extended before her. "Napoleons," she said, kicking off her shoes. Her face was glowing. Daddy and I clutched her in a three-way hug.

"Yes!" she said. "Yes! This little old homemaker, overqualified and underexperienced, has got herself a job."

She was so happy, she deserved a parade, bands, fireworks, cheerleaders. Napoleon Bonaparte's victories were pushovers compared to hers.

One of the agencies that specializes in executive secretaries and had snubbed her at first, got tired of having her come back and pester them, so, finally, to get rid of her, they sent her over to a big real estate firm in Paramus.

"I had to do it," she said. "Mr. Campbell, the yuppy personnel director, was so obnoxious I had to do it just to show him. 'Why do you want to leave your comfortable suburban life after all these years, Mrs. Warren, to enter the harried, competitive work world?'

"First I thought of saying, 'Sonny, it's none of your button-down, baby-boom business.' Which it really wasn't, but I wanted the job. So I smiled at him sweetly and blinked the old eyes and said, 'We need the money desperately, Mr. Campbell.' He was so appalled by my candor, he just sent me along to his assistant, Ms. Mudd. She was wearing a gray tailored suit cloned from mine. I wanted to say that to her, but she was grim. She tested me: shorthand, typing, dictaphone, and when I said I could use the word processor I was in!"

Now Daddy may not be tall but he is strong, strong enough to embrace her and whirl her all around the kitchen till both of them were dizzy.

When he set her down and turned back to save the keema, she said, "You understand it's not the greatest job in the world. I'm not chairperson of the board."

"Not yet," Daddy said.

"But we're really only in the beginning of this phase of our lives—"

"In the beginning—" Daddy echoed, offering her a tablespoonful of our delicious-smelling curry. "Remember everything starts with 'In the beginning . . .' Carole, where is that line from?"

All praise went to you-know-which English teacher who picks them right. His mind and Daddy's ran along parallel lines. "'Genesis,'" I said coolly, "The Old Testament starts that way.

> In the beginning God created the heaven and the earth. And the earth was without form, and void; and darkness was upon the face of the deep. And the Spirit of God moved upon the face of the waters.
> And God said, Let there be light; and there was light."

Daddy swung his right arm in a great, deferential arc of respect and bowed, deeply. "Wonderful!" he said. "Can you go on?"

I had to confess that was it.

"That's as much as I can remember, myself. Daughter, you are terrific."

There was only one appropriate response to that and everything that happened that evening. Amen. Amen. Amen!

CHAPTER 8

Money was on my mind every minute for the first time in my life. Or rather, absence of money, lack of it, was on my mind. Every step, every decision I made was influenced by whether or not I had money. Before, in the good old dentist days, I could always go ask my parents. Sometimes they said no, but mostly they said yes. There's a lot to be said for cavities and braces and periodic prophylaxsis (the prevention of disease by treatment; in other words, cleanings and check-ups).

Now I had no cash and no credit card, and I couldn't bring myself to ask Daddy for anything. Jim paid for my movies and popcorn once and I knew he was glad to do it, but I wasn't going to make a habit of that. He hated kids who sucked up to him because his family had money. Besides, he tried to take as little as possible from his parents, much less than they offered because he knew there were strings attached, so he didn't really have a lot to spend.

In addition, there was Gloria's constant brainwashing of Monique—who passed it along to me—about independence. "You have to learn how to make your own way," was Gloria's message. "Where would I be if I didn't have this interior decorating business? Thank God I stayed in school and finished."

Monique earned spending money baby-sitting many nights, but I really didn't know anything about kids. I wasn't sure I even liked them all that much. Truthfully, I was scared of them, especially the little ones. They seemed to be so fragile.

I needed a job desperately.

One good thing: lunches in school had definitely improved. I did my best with the pepperoni and cream cheese, and ham, and meatloaf. Monique brought winners like huge roast beef sandwiches on Jewish rye with caraway seeds. Another good thing about my empty pockets was that I couldn't buy Hershey bars; I was losing weight. Jim said I was looking lithe. (I had to go check the dictionary. It means pliant, supple, limber.) Ms. Porter, the track coach, watched me work out and yelled "Way to go, Carole." First time she called me by my first name.

Running laps with my partner, Angie Samuels, I thought a lot about my family's situation. Angie and I were paired by Ms. Porter early in the term, after she'd watched and timed all the runners. We're a good match; Angie and I pace each other well. But she's got greater staying power. It's not any kind of physical strength. She just works harder than anyone else on the team.

"So what's your secret, Angie?" I asked her. "You come to practice early, you leave late, and you work harder than anyone else. You can't want to win more than I do because that's what I want most in the world. What is it? What keeps you going when you can hardly breathe?"

Angie flashed a grin at my question. She's a slim graceful girl with gorgeous cheekbones, large brown eyes, a fairly dark skin, and perfect teeth. She's so pretty, she could model. I told her that once, but she put it down. "Who wants to earn a living that way? Dummy work. It must be so boring."

"You may have noticed that I happen to be black?" she said now.

"Yeah. I noticed," I said. "What kind of crazy answer is that?"

"It means I know there is no second chance. If Angie Samuels, who is a competent but not brilliant student, wants to go to a good college, Angie Samuels has to win an athletic scholarship to go. No scholarship, no first-rate college."

"Angie, I'm going to be competition," I said, and I told her about Daddy.

"That is some story. Seems as if people are never satisfied," she said.

"Well—my father finds dentistry a drag. A while ago you said the same thing about modeling."

"Yeah," she conceded. "I guess the thing is to do your choosing while you're young."

I nodded. "He made a mistake. He really wants to try acting and my mom thinks he should have the chance."

"What do you think?" She looked at me intently.

"Nobody asked me."

"I'm asking you."

"It's very inconvenient. But I guess he should try."

"Well, don't worry about competing with me. If I'm really good, plenty of schools will be courting me because I am a member of a minority. You are just plain old ordinary poor white."

She made me laugh.

"What's more," she added evilly, "those chocolate bars are slowing you down."

"No more. I'm too broke to buy them these days."

"Are you looking for work, Carole? The fast-food places on the mall all hire part time. Come to McDonald's with me."

I couldn't. I just couldn't. From Saturday shopper to hamburger seller? And what if Christa and Jean decided to go slumming and eat Big Macs for lunch? "I'll think about it. I've got a couple of other ideas."

"Like what?"

61

"Baby-sitting."

"No money in that. I find when I do it they usually pay the least they can. And sometimes they try to get dishes and housework done too. That makes me mad."

"I do have a chance for light housecleaning. Four hours a week, five bucks an hour."

"That's a good job. Not many part times like it here in Ashland for school kids. That's over the minimum."

"I hate cleaning."

"Know anyone who loves it?" Angie asked. "You're just too picky and fussy to be poor, Ms. Carole Warren. You better come down to earth like the rest of us earthlings. You think I *like* wearing that dumb uniform and serving hamburgers?"

She was right, of course. As I headed home, I made my decision. First thing, I called Jim and asked him to speak to his mother for me.

He was pleased. "You'll get to see the whole Dunham Museum, at last." He kept his voice low. "My father's soldiers and all the rare porcelains." In all the years I'd known him, I'd only been in the kitchen and the finished basement of his house. The rest of it was off-limits to kids. "I thought you hated housework, Carole."

"Who, me? Whatever gave you that impression? I love it. Dusting is my *thing*."

The receiver clattered out of his hand, but once he had everything under control again he assured me, "In that case, I think you just got yourself a job. I'll talk Mother into it."

Larry had really been happy when he heard the news about Mom's job. At the time, he was scrounging around for regular part-time work. Providence didn't have a lot to offer. Occasional bartending was not enough.

Then he called us. He had gotten a job and he loved it.

I wasn't at all sure I loved it.

"It's a regular part-time job here at the school," he said. "It pays well and I don't have to do a thing."

"Really?" Daddy said. "Sounds ideal. What kind of job is it?"

"The Art Department offers a course called Open Studio with Live Model. I—am the model."

I hooted. "Who would want to draw your ugly face?"

"It ain't my face, kid, though they can do that if they like."

Then it hit me. "Larry—you're not—you aren't—"

"Yes, I am. Mr. Centerfold himself."

"Larry!"

"It's an art class, Carole. Sex doesn't enter into it."

"Tell me about it."

"You high school kids are so immature. You don't understand art."

"How can you do it?" I whispered. "Aren't you embarrassed?"

"Listen," he said, "it's actually very hard work. I sit for long periods of time in a single position while twenty or so people sketch me. It's a studio course.

Three hours a session. You'd be amazed at how many itches and sniffles and aches I have in three hours. I take breaks but a lot of the time I don't move."

"Are you cold?"

"No. The studio is comfortably heated. It's a real good job and it's for the year."

"Don't write to anyone here in Ashland about it," I begged. "Please. Especially not to anyone in the high school, Larry."

"Relax," he said. "I'm only telling family."

I felt enormously grateful. "Thanks. So long, Beefcake."

Mom and Dad were not shocked or upset; they were amused. "You may be immortalized, son," Daddy said. "Some great artist will draw you and make you famous."

"I doubt it," Larry said. "The serious artists up here are at the Rhode Island School of Design, not at Brown. Besides, I've seen the drawings. No Rembrandts, no Cézannes around. Any resemblance between me and what they draw is purely coincidental."

That made me feel better. Providence, Rhode Island, is pretty far from Ashland and if the drawings didn't look like him no one would have to know.

I still thought he could wear a bikini, but Mom said no, there's no reason to be ashamed of the human body. True, but there's no reason to go around flaunting it either.

Again and again my family keeps surprising me.

"All over Europe," Daddy said, "there are nude beaches. When I'm a wealthy employed actor I'll take my family traveling to such a beach."

"I'll keep my eyes closed the whole time," I said.

"If you have any sense you'll peek," Mom said, laughing.

I wonder if I would.

CHAPTER

9

Well, it happened. Monique was really praying that it wouldn't happen, and then it did.

I had just hung up on Christa after lying to her, telling her I had a virus and I couldn't go mall cruising, I was sorry. As I stood folding sheets and trying to figure out the fastest, easiest, and neatest way to fold, in that order of importance, Monique called and asked if she could come over. "Sure," I said, figuring it must be a Number One Emergency from the whispery voice and the hour—early Saturday morning. "You'll find me in the basement folding laundry," I told her. "Come right down here."

She biked over, fast. Her face would have won the misery prize in any contest.

"You look like you lost your best friend," I said, "which isn't possible because I'm it."

"I lost my next-to-best friend," she said.

"Who's that?"

"The Jogger."

"Oh! I'm sorry, Monique."

"Me, too."

"He's gone for good? You're sure?"

She nodded.

"What happened? Do you know?"

"I was there through it all," she said glumly. "It was terrible. He took us out to dinner last night at Rinaldi's."

"That wasn't terrible," I said. "I bet you had the sausage special."

I was envious. Rinaldi's is a Neapolitan restaurant that just opened. Their specialty is individual dinner-plate size pizzas made to your order; anything—mushrooms, onions, green peppers, sausage—in any combination goes on them. They're incredible.

"Yeah. The Jogger ordered it all in Italian. I figured it would come out all wrong, but it didn't. You should have heard him. I even had two spumonis for dessert."

"Two?" I was silenced by the extravagance of this dinner.

"It was so good, in fact, it made everything worse."

"I don't see how, Monique. I figure if the world ends or something awful happens after I've eaten something great, well, at least I've had that much."

67

She shook her head. "It really was spoiled."

I didn't push it, but I am privately convinced that once you've eaten something up, whatever happens afterward can't affect it. How can it be spoiled? It was already enjoyed. I think I'll ask Doubting Thomas, my social studies teacher, what his opinion is. He loves philosophical questions. His favorite response to anything is "I doubt that."

"Tell me what happened," I urged.

"When we were all through eating, we were just sitting there and they were finishing off their wine and me my spumoni, and then suddenly Gloria wanted a cigarette. For a while now she's been working on it, cutting down and stopping and then starting again. Well, she didn't have any cigarettes on her because she's given them up this month. So she ordered a pack.

"'Please, Gloria,' the Jogger said, 'don't start again.' He told the waiter in Italian not to bring the cigarettes.

"Well, you know Gloria. She was in one of her independent moods. 'Bring the cigarettes,' she told the waiter. 'I'll pay for them myself.'"

"That was mean."

"The Jogger thought so too. It made him angry. 'You know I don't mind paying for anything you order, Gloria. It's just that cigarettes are deadly. And you were doing so well. I thought you had them licked.'

"She didn't answer him. When the waiter brought the cigarettes, she took out her wallet and paid for them. The Jogger asked for the check then and he said he was leaving. He stood up. He was pretty mad. I've never seen him mad before; he's always so good-natured, kidding Gloria and me. He moved up close to Gloria and bent over so the other customers couldn't hear—and he told her she had me to consider because she's a single parent, and she was selfish and childish."

"What'd she say?"

"She said she didn't need advice from anyone. She had managed fine thus far in her life, and she was an adult.

"He said maybe she hadn't managed quite so fine thus far in her life, that adulthood was not determined by age but by maturity and there she had some way to go."

"Wow!" I was impressed. *"Way to go*, Jogger."

"Yeah," Monique agreed desolately, "but it didn't do any good. Gloria was sore. I think maybe she was even sorry later, but she'll never admit it."

"He just walked out?"

"No. He came over to me and he bent down and told me that I was his friend too, not just Gloria's daughter, and any time I felt like jogging I could just give him a call. He also advised me to stay near open windows and do my best not to hang around and inhale when Gloria was killing herself. 'Don't let her kill you too,' he said, and he gave her one long sad look and then he walked out."

"Too bad. Monique, I'm really sorry."

"Yeah. I'd take him up on the jogging offer because he really is a friend and never once talked to me like he

69

thought I was just a dumb kid, but I can't call him up because it would be disloyal to Gloria."

"Maybe Gloria will cool off. Maybe she'll call him up and apologize in a few days."

"Over her dead body. Gloria doesn't ever apologize, especially when she knows she's in the wrong, because then she gets angry with herself for being stupid. She makes it up to you, but she doesn't apologize. So it's good-bye Jogger." Monique sighed. "And you know what the worst part of this is? Not only do we lose the Jogger as our friend, but Gloria will begin having boyfriends again, the ones that cheer her up. And you know what they're like."

She was so down she stayed and helped me fold the rest of the laundry just so she wouldn't have to go right back home. *That* is down.

CHAPTER 10

If I astonished myself by agreeing to do housework for money, apparently I astonished Mrs. Dunham more. She was more than astonished; she was scandalized. Jim was waiting for me at the locker-room door as I headed in at three o'clock. He repeated the conversation to me word for word.

"'Mother, I've found someone who would like to have the part-time housework job here. Carole would like it.'

"'Carole? What Carole? Not Carole Warren, that little girl who used—'

"'That Carole Warren.'

"'Whatever are you talking about, James? She's a professional's daughter.'

"'Mother, she—'

71

"'Her father is a dentist. Dentists' daughters don't dust.' She smiled. 'What's that called again?'

"'Alliteration, Mother. Carole is not a dentist's daughter any more. At least, not exactly.'

"'Whatever are you talking about, James? How can she stop being a dentist's daughter?'

"'Her father isn't doing dentistry any more. Except on Sundays!'

"'Sundays?' She looked worried. 'Get Rhonda to put her palm on your forehead, James, and see if you have a fever.'

"'Dr. Warren plans to handle emergency cases for other dentists on Sundays. During the week he's going to become an actor.'

"'James, have you been experimenting with narcotics? I read such dreadful stuff about marijuana and cocaine—'

"'Mother, you know I wouldn't.'

"'I do know, dear, but you have an inquiring mind. And you are acting so strangely.'

"'Mother, Dr. Warren has always wanted to be an actor. When I went by there Saturday night, he tried Antony's speech on me. You know, from the play *Julius Caesar*. "My heart is in the coffin there with Caesar . . ."

"'*Julius Caesar*? The poor man must be very troubled. Be careful if you go there again. One never knows—'

"'Dr. Warren is not crazy. He just loves acting. He

wandered into dentistry by mistake, so now he's wandering out. He wants to give the stage a try.'

"'That is the wildest story I have ever heard, James. Dr. Warren is a grown man with a family and responsibilities. What does his wife say to all this?'

"'She thinks it's great. She has just gone back to work so he can try this.'

"'It sounds most peculiar to me.'

"'May Carole have the job here?'

"'I don't see why not if she's careful with the porcelains and your father's miniatures. One good thing, we know she's honest. Tell her to phone Rhonda this afternoon and set up an appointment with me.'

"So," Jim finished, "call Rhonda after you're done running."

I used the pay phone in the dressing room after I'd showered. Rhonda and I worked out the schedule, Tuesdays and Thursdays from four-thirty to six-thirty. I'd finish track and I'd bike over there. "I haven't seen you in so long, Carole," Rhonda said. "I bet you've grown something remarkable."

"I'm as tall as Jim."

"But prettier. That boy has almost given up eating. Jim is having one hard time."

"I know," I said.

"Well, enough of that. You come Thursday. Mrs. Dunham will be here and she'll talk to you for about a minute. That's all."

"You going to be my boss, Rhonda?"

73

She loved that. "Always was. Always told you what to do and what not to do in the playground. What a nice little kid you used to be."

"Still am. Only not so little."

"See you Thursday, Carole. Leave your butterfingers home."

Rare luck! I ran into Christa and Jean just as I'd *finished* the phone call. Two minutes earlier and they would have heard it all! They were both wearing gorgeous new Shaker knit cotton sweaters; Christa's was pale yellow and Jean's was aqua. The raglan sleeves were pushed up to midarm. Neat sweaters.

"We've been missing you at the mall," Christa said. "Last Saturday we had a terrific day. Bloomie's is featuring these sensational new cotton knits."

"We ended up getting a couple each," Jean said. "Different colors so we can trade."

"You both look terrific," I said.

"Thanks." Jean smiled and picked imaginary lint off the sweater. "They have other colors too, white, pink, royal blue, red, and black."

"After shopping we went to see the latest *Police Academy* movie and then we had Szechwan food until we burst—chicken with walnuts and that wild garlic eggplant you love," Christa said. "We ordered it in your honor."

"Thanks," I said.

"Next Saturday when we go we can stop there first

74

with you, and you can look at the sweaters for your-self," Jean offered. "You won't be able to resist them."

Christa didn't seem to think that was such a hot idea. Usually we rotated the stores we went to, so we didn't look at the same stuff two weeks in a row.

I always knew that Jean was a nicer person than Christa, maybe not strong—she's a follower—but a lit-tle more sensitive. "Thanks, Jean," I said. "I'm sorry, but I won't be going with you any more on Saturdays."

The two of them gaped at me as if spots had suddenly appeared. "Wha-a-at?" they squealed in unison.

"I won't be going mall cruising on Saturdays any-more."

"Ever?" Christa gasped. "You're grounded forever? What did you do?"

At this point I had to make a serious choice. I could tell them the truth right off, or I could make up a lie to protect myself. Quickly, I reviewed mentally a list of possibilities. I'm seeing a shrink because I'm a chocoholic; I'm taking a karate course, so when I'm a black belt my parents will allow me to go into New York City alone; I'm doing extra running with Angie. Any one of these would have kept them busy for a while. Wondering, checking. Credit-Card Carole could have lied with the ease of Pinocchio. Their good opinion had been important to her. But now I was Carole, daughter of an itinerant actor (Oh Brutal Blake, behold my learn-ing!), and an executive secretary. I was Carole the duster.

"I don't have a charge card anymore."

"What did you *do*?" Christa was fascinated.

I hated to disappoint her. "Nothing. It's just that—my family doesn't have the money for that sort of thing."

"But your father is a dentist," Jean said. Hot news.

"No more. He's giving it up."

"Someone's suing him for malpractice," Christa guessed. "He pulled the wrong tooth." She grinned a mean little grin.

"No. He's going to be an actor."

"You're kidding," Jean said.

"No. He's always wanted to be one."

The two of them looked at each other goggle-eyed.

"You've been sniffing some of his ether," Christa accused.

I denied it. One good thing about Daddy not being a dentist anymore. No more ether jokes.

"What will he act in? Fluoride commercials?" Christa was hot today.

"Plays. He hopes to find something in New York. Off Broadway or on Broadway. He doesn't exactly know."

"I can't believe it," Christa said. "How can he be so selfish? I mean—here you are in high school and all, and suddenly your father pulls this?"

"He's always loved acting. He wants a chance at it before he's too old." I found myself defending him. "He's a wonderful actor."

Christa couldn't see it. She shook her head. "My father better not try that. Of course he never would. He likes being an actuary."

"What's an actuary?"

"Something to do with insurance rates."

"Sounds fascinating."

She gave me a dirty look. "Your father ought to grow up. When he was young and going to school, he had his chance. Now it's over. It's your turn. Why don't you tell him it's the younger generation's turn now?"

"Christa, he's only forty-two. That's not very old. He's entitled to another try if that's what he wants."

"Then when is your turn?"

I didn't have an answer. I shrugged. "I have to go now." I hopped on my bike and pedaled away fast, glad to leave them behind. We had not been close friends. We liked to do the same thing—shop. But I always knew, secretly, that we were not *real* friends. I settled for less with them, and, in a way, it was dishonest. I gave less too. I won't do that again, spend time with people I am not really fond of and pretend I am having a sensational time with them. I was using them and they were using me.

Daddy's career change was certainly causing what Doubting Thomas liked to refer to as "endless ripples."

Our daily routine quickly became fixed. Each weekday morning, Daddy got up first and showered and dressed very carefully. Once he was finished in the bathroom he became our alarm clock. "Rise and shine," he'd call. "Rise and shine." He took the line from *The Glass Menagerie*.

"I'll rise but I won't shine," I answered, from the same play. Actually, the character in the play hated to be awakened that way. But I didn't mind.

Daddy put a denim shirt on over his good clothes and set up the coffee and started breakfast preparations. Afterward, he and I cleared the table and did the dishes so Mom could get right on her way. While, at first, this middle-aged Mr. Mom routine felt weird—as if this could not be real life—very quickly we settled into this new pattern so that I hardly noticed it.

It seems as though the most extraordinary changes can be absorbed so that they become everyday normal life. For months, Monique's mother and Monique too had been running early mornings with the Jogger. That was the way most of the Shapiros' days started. Now when they got up, Gloria did an hour of silent meditation. Monique would have loved to go out running, but she didn't out of loyalty to Gloria, so she was doing aerobics to a tape in her bedroom.

At our house immediately after breakfast, Mom took off for work. Daddy, with portfolio, caught a bus into the city to make rounds. He saw himself as a character actor, both serious and comic, middle-aged but able to do older or somewhat younger parts. He was a fine mimic and he had an excellent ear for accents. He had played Otto Frank in *The Diary of Anne Frank*, and Dr. Van Helsing in *Dracula*. He really was versatile. "Well, let's see if anyone is looking for George today," he'd say as he went out the door. George is the drunken unhappy college professor in *Who's Afraid of Virginia Woolf?* Daddy had been a smash in the part. (Our old neighbor, Mrs. Monroe, couldn't get over how believable he was as a drunkard. "You sure you were acting?" she kept saying. "It looked *so real*.") Somedays instead of George, Daddy hoped they'd be needing the Stage Manager for *Our Town*, or one of Shakespeare's clowns, or Cyrano, or Lear, or Tevye in *Fiddler on the*

Roof. Anyone. Daddy was prepared to be anyone on stage.

Most nights he came home tired but not discouraged. There was something about this dream that sustained him. I could see it. In the weeks right after he'd stopped being a full-time dentist, he seemed younger to me.

He'd come home beat, but later in the evening he'd bounce back. Possibilities were out there. He talked about them after dinner. He studied *Variety* and *Show Business* and the other trade papers, reading ads aloud and making notes, endless notes.

At first, he didn't get more than one reading for any part. First readings are very preliminary. And the few people who bothered to look at his composite and his resumé—mostly secretaries—were not impressed by community theater credits earned in New Jersey. "If it's not New York, it doesn't count," Daddy said once, wearily. "Out-of-town experience counts for nothing. They look for on Broadway or maybe—maybe—good Off Broadway experience. It wouldn't matter if I'd done five hundred parts in community theater."

Mom soothed him and tried to encourage him. "You'll get a break," she said. "You've got to get a break. Everyone has to start somewhere." He didn't answer, but next morning he was his old rise-and-shine optimistic self.

Very quickly he figured out where to be and when. There was a bulletin board at Actors' Equity that announced the specific times allotted for open casting.

Daddy made sure he was on the spot in good time. At least he got more chances. And on those days when he read, he came home all excited and he and Mom dissected every word and gesture and breath and sign that occurred during the interview. Then there was the wait for the callback. There were several callbacks but they didn't develop into anything.

"I don't know anyone," Daddy said. "In this business it's crucial to have contacts. But I'm not going to give up. I know I'm a good actor."

One night he came home, his face gray with weariness and sadness. We could see right off that something had happened. Neither Mom nor I asked. We ate dinner quietly, and we cleaned up afterward. Then, later, in the living room, he told us about it.

"I was going along West Forty-sixth Street heading toward Actors' Equity when a really seedy-looking, skinny panhandler stopped me. The guy was skeletal. 'Hey, bo,' he said, 'you an actor?'

"I nodded. 'How did you know?'

"'I can always tell. It's the dream in your step. I'm an actor myself. Pretty good too. I studied in London. In 1979 I did *Richard the Third* in the Minnesota Regional Theater.'

"And right there he launched into Richard! He was dirty, his skin scabby, his long hair knotted every which way. But he had the bluest eyes I've ever seen, piercing blue eyes. He was no drunk—just a defeated man. He had no shoes. There he stood on West Forty-sixth Street among the tourists, barefooted, acting.

'Slave, I have set my life upon a cast
And I will stand the hazard of the die.
I think there be six Richmonds in the field;
Five have I slain today instead of him.
A horse! a horse! my kingdom for a horse!'

"He wasn't bad either. 'Can you spare some change for a meal?' he asked me. I gave him a couple of dollars. 'Thanks, much,' he said. 'I wish you luck if you stick with it. I stuck with it too long. I just couldn't let go. God bless you.'"

Daddy shook his head vigorously trying to shake the memory. "I have to give myself a time limit. That's what I have to do."

"No, you don't," Mom said quietly.

"I don't think you should set a time limit now," I said. "Remember 'In the beginning . . .'?"

Daddy gave me a hug, a full, Broadway center-stage, third-act hug. "I have what that poor fellow didn't have."

"A horse?" I looked around.

"Not a horse. I've got the crucial ingredient, the impenetrable shield. You guys and Larry."

This was followed by a really sloppy finale.

CHAPTER
12

I didn't go to the movies with Jim on Saturday night. "Next week," I promised him, "when I can pay my own way." He didn't try to persuade me; he understood.

Dusting Day finally arrived. I had no credit card and no money—none—and I couldn't bring myself to ask my parents for any. Hiring me to do housework was about as appropriate as hiring Clint Eastwood for the infant room of a day care center. Nobody was less suited to do housework than Credit-Card Carole. But in Ashland there is no industry, just a few small stores; if Mrs. Dunham hired me, I'd be lucky.

Lucky: a *paradox,* an exact contradiction (courtesy Doubting Thomas, whose favorite word it was). Lucky to get the job; unlucky because I disliked what it entailed. My part-time situation was parallel to Daddy's

83

full-time situation. He could earn money as a dentist, plenty of money, but it didn't give him pleasure.

Jim and I had decided that it would be best if he were not around when his mother interviewed me, so he stayed away that afternoon. Rhonda let me in, the same Rhonda, in a soft beige uniform, a bit heavier, direct black eyes, hair graying now. She gave my shoulder a friendly clasp.

Mrs. Dunham, a frail, slightly stooped woman with carefully waved blond hair, was wearing a tailored black silk dress and real jewelry. I mean diamonds. Ring. Choker. Earrings. They glowed in the dim room. She was very pleasant if rather vague.

Jim had explained about his mother to me long ago when I asked why she was never around. She's asthmatic and has never been very well. She has to rest a lot. Jim was born late in her life, so she has always regarded him as a sort of miracle. She would give him the moon if she could. That he takes so little from her and his father and that he gets along so badly with his father hurts her deeply. The two of them do their best to shield her, but Jim says she knows. "She's sick, not stupid. She understands she can't change things, so she doesn't admit to them. But she knows a lot."

Mrs. Dunham was sitting on a long white linen-upholstered couch, resting when Rhonda showed me in. "Good afternoon, Carole. James has told me something of your family's—delicate—circumstances," she began graciously.

"Not really delicate, Mrs. Dunham. Unusual. My father has given up his dental practice except for Sundays to pursue another career."

"So James said." She seemed to be rather embarrassed by what Daddy had done. "Well, we will be glad to have your services. We need careful dusting of the collections on our upper floor. The objects are extremely fragile and quite valuable, so it is a time-consuming and responsible job. Two afternoons should take care of it all nicely. Do you know anything about porcelains?"

"A little. My mother loves them. She has some Wedgwood and Spode. I even own one piece that I got for my birthday, the Royal Doulton figure, Sairey Gamp. She stands on my dresser."

That was the closest I came to seeing Mrs. Dunham come awake from the pleasant detachment she seemed to live in. She really loved her porcelains. She leaned forward a little. "I had no idea!" she said. "So few young people care about beauty these days. James has no interest at all."

Not in porcelains, I thought, but he is interested in beauty. He finds it in music. Of course I said nothing.

"I'm confident you will do a careful job. Rhonda will show you around." She pressed a little button set in the rim of the coffee table, and Rhonda materialized in a minute. "Good-bye, dear," Mrs. Dunham said, and, leaning back, she closed her eyes.

Rhonda took me by the hand and led me upstairs. "Good to see you, Carole," she said softly. "It's time for you to stop growing. You're tall enough."

"Tell my genes, Rhonda. I take after my mother. I've got no say in it."

She nodded. "That's the way it is. But you still have to try. Concentrate. Keep telling yourself no more, no more. Walk small.

"We're going to their display rooms now, the War Room and the Dish Room I call them. Nobody else calls them that—except Jim—so don't you call them that around here or there'll be trouble." She winked.

We had arrived. We entered a vast white gallery with brightly colored Persian rugs covering the floor. The walls were filled with hanging dishes, and there was a gigantic breakfront with choice pieces displayed, creamers and various size bowls, cups, and saucers. Then there were glass shelves, rows and rows of them built into the walls, on which platters and figures stood. Gorgeous pieces. It *was* a museum.

"When you come here to work, come in the kitchen door and pick up a snack before you start. Just like old times in the playground," Rhonda said. I squeezed her hand gratefully. Her brownies had more chocolate in them than Hershey bars. When Jim and I were kids, she never fed him without taking care of me.

"You just take your time up here." She showed me a hidden closet in which there was a bag of soft cloths. "Move very slowly because these dishes cost and no matter what fancy name Mrs. Dunham calls them, Crack and Break is their real name. Before I graduated out of this job, I hated it the most of anything. I'd rather wash windows and clean toilets any day." She smiled at me. "I don't mean to put down your job."

"I'm not crazy about dusting either, Rhonda, but I need the money."

"That's a reason," she said. "That's *the* reason. Now let me show you Mr. Dunham's collection." Another vast room, more shelves, and there they were, row after row, exquisite little men in various uniforms, and horses and cannon. Some were set out on the green felt surface of a huge rectangular table. Well, my father might be considered strange because of his career behavior, but Mr. Dunham wouldn't win the All-American-Sanity prize either, I concluded. Surely there were more meaningful ways for him to spend his time—and his money.

I looked at Rhonda. She had a poker face. She had worked for the Dunhams for a very long time, and she was loyal. She wouldn't talk against them to me. I thought I saw a glint in her eye that showed she was amused, that showed she thought them oddball. But she didn't say one single word against them.

So I began to dust. And I dusted and I dusted and I dusted. Two hours felt like ten hours. I was so scared I would break something, my hands actually trembled. But I didn't drop anything.

Many of the plates were extremely beautiful and so delicate they were almost weightless. Others were amazingly heavy. I memorized some of the names, Royal Crown, Derby, Haviland, and Rosenthal. Mom would absolutely drool when she heard about all the great porcelains I'd handled.

The miniature soldiers were easier. Rhonda had said I should pick up each one by the base, hold it firmly, and gently wipe it. No transferring from hand to hand. Use the ladder for the higher shelves. Take, dust, replace.

Ten dollars an afternoon, twenty dollars a week. I thought about Larry posing nude, itching and unable to scratch. I thought about Daddy walking about the city following up every lead, and Mom sitting at her word processor—she apparently was good at it—and dealing with Mr. Button-Down Campbell and Ms. Mudd, and I felt proud of myself. A peculiar pride. For the first time in my life, I was earning my own money.

There was plenty of time to reflect, and with reflections come resolutions. I made them by the platterful. When I have my own home, I am going to cultivate dust like a crop. Never, no never, am I going to wield a dustcloth. Perhaps penicillin or some other great and beneficial mold will grow out of my undisturbed dust.

And I shall never buy a single inessential object that needs care.

What about the figure of Sairey Gamp on my dresser? Well, that was a birthday gift from my mother before I made this resolution. I can't help having that. Anyway, Sairey looks better with dust. Like an antique.

CHAPTER 13

I was partner to two separate crises on the same day and neither crisis was mine; I mean, I *only* had an unemployed father. That was nothing compared to what Jim and Monique were dealing with.

I knew that Gloria had found a new boyfriend. He'd been around for only a short time, but Monique couldn't stand him. That was unusual for Monique. Before this guy, Al, appeared, she had always done her best to stay out of Gloria's personal life. Live and let live. She figured Gloria was old enough to make her own judgments. And her own mistakes.

"The morning of the day Gloria met him, I broke the magnifying mirror," Monique told me.

"So?" We were holding huge heros, prosciutto and Swiss cheese, provided by me. I was really getting good at this brown-bag deal. All it took was a little adding to the Saturday grocery list. I was eager to begin eating.

"So?"

"Well, if breaking a regular mirror is bad luck then breaking a magnifying mirror is a disaster."

"That's crazy. He can't be that bad."

"He's that bad, Carole."

"What's he like?"

"Three guesses."

I pointed to her sandwich so that she'd start to eat, and I took a bite of mine. I considered the problem. "He's good looking?" I said.

"Yes. In a Sylvester Stallone kind of way."

"Mmm. Sounds promising."

"For what? My stepfather or a member of the mob?"

"Good sandwich, eh?" I said.

She nodded. "Guess again."

"Blow-dried hair?"

"Right. And flashy suits, padded and tight-fitted to show the bod. Big shoulders. And sideburns."

"Not sideburns?"

"Yes. Honest-to-god sideburns."

"That's too much," I said.

"There's more. He wears satin ties and Gucci shoes. And he drives a cream sports car, an Alfa Romeo, he told me, as if I cared."

"Well, Gloria could teach him to dress better and not overdo the discotheque style. If that's all you've got against him, it's not *so* terrible. He really doesn't sound so bad to me."

"He doesn't sound so bad to Gloria either. In fact, she's nuts about him. When I told her he makes me feel uncomfortable and I couldn't give her a concrete reason why, she said I was being unfair and judgmental. I don't mean to be. But I just have this powerful weird feeling that he is off-key somehow."

"Maybe it's because you liked the Jogger so much. He had a very different style."

Monique smiled. "That's true. I did like him awfully. But he had absolutely *no* style. That was his style."

"I think he was the best Gloria's come up with so far."

Monique nodded vehemently.

"Can you pin down your feelings about this Al any better?"

She really was at a loss. "He has the sneakiest smile. And he just smiles all the time as if it's fixed on his face. And he laughs too loud, and he calls me 'Honey.'"

"That's not enough to hate him. He sounds annoying but not terrible."

"And whenever he laughs, it's loud."

I shrugged.

"I know, I know," she said woefully. "And, to make it worse, he's always buying me Toblerones and bringing me the latest *People* or *Rolling Stone*. He goes out of his way to be nice to me." She was desperate to make me understand. "Maybe it's because he's a salesman and he says everything in the same phony too-sincere way, as if he cared so much when you know he couldn't care less about whatever you're talking about. 'How's school?' he always asks me. When I start to tell him about Doubting Thomas and the Civil War and his theory about the Carpetbaggers, or about Blake and word origins, I can see his eyes creeping around the room and his fingers drumming on the chair arm. He doesn't want to hear any answer."

"Where did she meet him?"

"I told you, he sold her a used car."

"It'll pass, Monique. Give it time. Relax. You know Gloria. She's no fool. If he's a phony, she'll find out. She just likes to have a good time. He'll move on after a while, and she'll find someone else you'll like better."

Monique chewed for a while, thoughtful and silent. "Do you believe in intuition?"

"I don't know."

"I believe in intuition. Woman's intuition. And my intuition tells me that Al is all sleaze, and Gloria's going to get badly hurt. I'd like to save her."

"Come on, Monique. You're carrying this too far. The guy hasn't really done anything."

"She's the only mother I have, Carole." Her green eyes were blocked by tears. I offered her my paper napkin.

"As I see it," I said, "there's not much you can do. Just stay on top of it and see what happens."

She nodded and blew her nose.

I was sorry my heroic sandwiches were so little noticed because of the crisis, but I would do them again soon. "Keep me posted," I said. "Anything I can do . . ."

92

"Nothing anyone can do. Gloria says people have to make their own mistakes. And she is."

About ten that night I was trying to do my homework—while thinking about this guy Al and the question of intuition—when the phone rang, and it was Jim for me. "Come for a walk," he said. "I know it's late, but I need to talk."

Oddly, once he'd set up my dusting interview, he had almost disappeared. He spent many hours off in the school music room practicing the cello. I knew he was having one of his bad times because the troubles in South Africa were getting worse. The newspapers were filled with terrible pictures and stories: children killed, women beaten, and mass arrests. On campuses all over the United States, students were demonstrating against doing business with the white South African government. They wanted their colleges to divest. They blocked lecture halls and built shantytowns; they passed petitions; they got arrested. Some schools did divest; some would not; some students kept trying to change things.

That was what Jim wanted most: to be able to affect things, to change things just a little. What he really wanted was for his father to divest, personally, and to advise his clients to do likewise. His father thought that was ludicrous. His job was to earn money for his investors and to maintain his personal portfolio profitably. The Dunhams had been respected bankers for three generations.

I was right. They had had another of their fierce arguments. Jim repeated it to me, bitterly.

"The blacks would be the first to suffer from the destruction of the economy," his father argued. "And that's what divestment would do."

"It's wrong to support that government."

"It's not an admirable government, I agree, but that's not our affair. Many blacks support the same position I do on tactics. Chief Buthelezi, the leader of six million Zulus sees it my way. Anti-apartheid whites in South Africa, like Helen Suzman, who's been fighting apartheid for years, see it my way. Why can't you, my son, see it?"

"Bishop Tutu doesn't," Jim argued. "Other ministers and priests don't."

"Can't you see that divestment is self-defeating?" his father asked wearily. "It destroys the one weapon the blacks are able to muster—the power to strike, to withdraw a skilled labor force in an economy that needs their skills."

"It's immoral to do business with that government."

"Morality is not relevant here, James."

"Morality is always relevant. I learned that in church."

His father was baffled. "It's not as simple as that. And you are too young to deal with all the issues."

Jim was trembling by the time he got through retelling this conversation. "That's how it ends each time. I'm too young, too young, too young!"

I held on to his arm tightly. "I think I understand. It

is terrible. But your father is right that it's not simple. In fact, even I see that it's too complicated for your simple answer."

He stopped walking and turned to stare at me. "You too?"

"Jim, you got me a job working in your house, and I'm being paid with your father's money. And Rhonda has been your maid all your life, and she gets paid with your father's money. What about that? If it's dirty money, how can any of us take it? Should I quit? Should Rhonda? Are you purer than we are?"

He was very pale in the moonlight, his face gaunt. "It's not the same. He's *my father*."

"All I'm saying is it's very complicated. We didn't make the world, and we aren't responsible for all its ugliness."

"But we have to try to change it."

"Agreed. But first we have to learn how. As Thomas keeps telling us in social studies, half-baked world changers do a lot of damage."

"So I'm to live like a fat cat while all those people are suffering and dying."

"You could never live like a fat cat. But there's not much that's meaningful that you can do now, in high school, in Ashland. You have to study and learn enough to make changes. You have to wait till it's your time."

"I don't know if I can, Carole. I just don't know if I can."

"If Nelson Mandela could live in jail all these years, if

he could survive and wait and believe, you have to learn how to wait too."

Jim put his arms around me and there in the bright moonlight he held me close and kissed me, my first real long absolutely grown-up kiss. His mouth was amazingly gentle but firm. It lasted forever. It was a wonderful kiss. It healed him for then, at least. We didn't say another word; we just walked very close to one another, like Siamese twins joined at the hip, through the bright night.

I prayed that night. I don't pray so often, but I prayed for Monique and for Jim. They needed help, more help than one friend could give them. They needed big help.

CHAPTER 14

Days and more days passed and then they turned into weeks. Each evening Daddy would come home with his face lined and tired, his pace slow. He and Mom or he and I would do something quick about dinner; we'd have hamburgers or chili con carne or chuck steak. Many nights I was salad girl and I learned pretty fast how bean sprouts or tofu or croutons could make a difference. Iceberg lettuce is so nothing without trimming. It became kind of a game. I read the supermarket circular and added new ingredients so the salads wouldn't be boring: mushrooms, leeks, romaine, capers, escarole, artichoke hearts, anchovies. My parents said that during the day and particularly on the way home at night they looked forward to my salads.

Nobody even once suggested that I be chief cook. And I wasn't exactly dying to spend my time alone in the kitchen when I could be watching MTV or listening to records. Especially since I was already spending four hours a week chasing the Dunham dust. But my mother worked till five o'clock and my father walked endlessly all day long. So one afternoon when I got home first, I figured I would start dinner.

I had about as much experience cooking a whole dinner as Boy George has playing football, but I decided to give it a try. What could I make? The only thing defrosted was a package of chopped meat. I snooped around in the kitchen closets and in the refrigerator. The answer was obvious. Meat sauce and pasta. We had boxes of number eight spaghetti. (Number eight is very skinny. I got to wondering what one through seven were like.) We had canned tomatoes and purée on hand.

The recipes were right there on the spaghetti box and on the can of purée. I began. I peeled and cut onions. I cried. I peeled garlic. I squashed it in the garlic press. I browned the onion, garlic, and meat in olive oil. It smelled divine. Every other minute I ran back to read the instructions. Salt, oregano, basil, tomatoes. I checked to be sure all the ingredients were included. I left the sauce to simmer and set the table while the water for the pasta was coming to a boil.

Then I began to clean up.

How could I ever ever ever have used so many

dishes and pots and bowls and kitchen utensils? The kitchen was so cluttered with stuff there was no open surface. Every counter and the sink and the stove were covered. It was unbelievable what a mess I had made.

I counted as I washed; I had used twenty-three dishes, utensils, pots, and other kitchen paraphernalia. Twenty-three must be a world record.

My parents were so grateful and so flattering—we ate every bit of everything—it was worth it. "This dinner is a gourmet's dream," Daddy said, and Mom nodded, her mouth full. I planned to cook again. More carefully though. I'd set a maximum on the number of cooking tools I'd use, and I'd stay within it. Five seemed a good number but a little unrealistic. I determined to keep it under ten.

Each evening as we ate, Daddy would tell us where he'd been and what he'd tried out for and who he'd seen. Lots of famous actors and actresses wandered in and out of the places he waited in: Al Pacino, Geraldine Fitzgerald, Matthew Broderick, Jason Robards, Jr., Dustin Hoffman, Kevin Kline. He went everywhere, uptown, downtown, out to Brooklyn. He followed every lead. A couple of times he was pretty sure he was close to getting a part. He waited for the callbacks. They didn't come.

After dinner, he'd collapse into his armchair. Next morning he was up as usual, and he was fresh and hopeful once again.

But nothing really happened. The pile of compositesresumés was dwindling and still nothing really happened. I was worried. How much disappointment can a person take? If being a dentist made him sick, *not being* an actor would surely make him worse. I talked to Mom about it privately on Sunday morning when Daddy was safely out of the way in his office.

"Oddly," Mom said, "his blood pressure is down and he hasn't had a chest pain since he started looking for acting jobs."

"But he's so tired at night he can barely make it home."

"He does come home exhausted, but sore feet are rarely fatal." Mom smiled at me and smoothed the tangle I had teased into my hair. (She's not used to what she calls "irregular hair.") "Carole, Daddy is doing what he's always wanted to do. At least, he's trying to do it. I think he's going to make it. But even if he doesn't, he has got to try."

I gave it a lot of thought. Deep thought. I don't really understand how people detour in their lives so they go off in directions they really didn't mean to. Once I know what I want to be, I am going to go that way and that way only, and any obstacles that block my path better move or I'll crush them.

I wonder when I'll know for sure. I already know specific things I don't want to be. I don't want to be a dentist. It's an honorable calling, as Daddy says, but not for me. It has no glamour. And I can't be an engineer or an architect because I am math blind. My bridges and buildings would collapse. I guess one morning I'll wake up and I'll just know the destiny of Carole Warren. Nurse? Teacher? Great chef? Owner of a *chocolaterie*? It will be there in my head. It had better be there in my head.

On Sundays Daddy really bustled. If he told the exchange he was going to be available on a certain Sunday, he became the emergency dentist for the whole area. It seemed as if all the others did not want to be disturbed on weekends. Many dentists in surrounding towns used Daddy as their backup. Sudden toothaches were the most common complaint, but complicated emergency cases called, too—like the man who swallowed his gold tooth. I won't tell what Daddy's advice to him was; it was sensible but indelicate.

"I don't mind this Sunday dentistry," Daddy said. "It's sort of nice to be available when people need help and there's no one else on hand."

There was not a lot of money around, but we were managing, Mom said, and Daddy continued to be hopeful. I hated seeing him come home each night defeated. If only some producer would agree to give him a part just once. For a short run. Just to let him know that he did have talent and the professional world recognized it. Because he *did* have talent. Onstage he could make an audience laugh or cry or hate him or love him or pity him. He deserved his chance. I didn't say it out loud, but I thought about it incessantly. Is one chance too much to ask for a terrific actor? After all those years he'd waited? Surely he should be allowed one chance.

Then, one night it happened!

He came home carrying a bouquet of red roses for Mom and one lovely pink rose for me. He had a part. Luck was with him. As usual, a freaky thing, luck.

He was Bogie again. A small Off Broadway company was doing *Play It Again, Sam* and the actor playing Bogie, as well as his understudy, had come down with chicken pox! Daddy was there, his composite right in hand with the wonderful picture of him in his trench coat as Bogie. "I did it without the book," Daddy said. "We ran through the whole thing, then the director asked me if I was free to open tomorrow night."

"What did you say, Daddy?"

"I hesitated for about one millionth of a minute and then I said I thought I could get out of my previous engagement."

"You didn't?"

"I did. I actually did." Daddy was a madman whirling about the living room. "Of course I got comps for anyone who wants to come."

It was a school night, but who cared? Larry had an Italian history exam the next day; he wanted to cut his exam and come down, but Daddy said no, come on the weekend. "You've seen my Bogart," he said. "By the weekend I'll really have the part polished."

The theater was a converted garage on Bleecker Street. It was shabby and not very large, but it had these huge classy blow-ups of great scenes from plays on all the lobby walls. The place was jammed, the audience wildly enthusiastic. Some of them were relatives and friends of the cast; they really loved it. The whole company was very good; it made me wonder why they were Off Broadway.

And Daddy? Daddy was terrific. It's just a small part, but he was so perfect—he had become Bogart! The lisp, the intonation, the five o'clock shadow, the way he walked. He was amazing.

During intermission I heard an elderly lady with very white face powder and cherry red lipstick say to her equally elderly male companion, "That Bogart is really Bogart! It's uncanny."

"That's my father," I told her.

"You must be very proud." She smiled at Mom and me.

"We are," Mom said.

"You bet," I agreed. Nice old lady. Good taste.

The play was scheduled to run for two months, and Daddy was earning the minimum Equity salary. There were seven o'clock Sunday night performances, but, happily, no Sunday matinees; so he started his dentistry earlier and he worked fanatically all day long till it was time to go to the theater. He said he was not in the least tired. He was invigorated.

Larry hitchhiked home on the weekend and Mom and I went again, with him, to see the play, taking along Monique and Jim. For those couple of hours the

103

two of them escaped the family troubles they were enmeshed in. Woody Allen is a genius!

But, though all the world's a stage, or so Shakespeare said, the stage is not the world. As we drove home, me happy and very proud, I sat between my two silent friends in the dark car and I knew we were all three of us worrying about what was in store for them.

CHAPTER 15

Something new in Ashland. An anti-apartheid table was set up on the sidewalk in front of our high school. Angie and the few other black kids took turns running it at first, and then after a major marathon argument with Jim and some other concerned whites who said the blacks were being racist if they wouldn't take help, it was agreed that all kinds of kids could take turns. So they did, whites, Koreans, Indians, Japanese. Ashland is close enough to New York City to draw all kinds of people. The only catch is that they have to be able to afford homes here.

What were they doing at the table? Two things:

One, they were collecting signatures on petitions asking the president and Congress to impose strong sanctions on the Pretoria government.

Two, they were collecting donations in a huge locked metal box to send to South Africa to be used in the struggle.

I volunteered a couple of my free periods. Angie was glad to have me. I even talked myself into parting with several dollars. (That was a struggle. I had earned those dollars *dusting*.)

I had never seen Jim so excited. He seemed to be there at the table day and night. And if away from it, he could talk of nothing else. *He was doing something*, at last. "It's not much, I know," he said, "but it is something. Rhonda gave me ten dollars for the box this morning. 'You sure?' I asked her. 'That is one stupid question,' she said. She was right. It was a stupid question. I'm amazed at how many people stop, and read the petition, and sign it, and contribute," he said. "I'm just amazed."

I was so glad to see him out of the dumps. Angie told me he was incredible at the table; few pedestrians could get by him. In fact, Jim had to be curbed literally. The group vetoed his going out into traffic and stopping cars. We were afraid his enthusiasm for the cause had destroyed all caution and common sense.

Monique, on the other hand, was looking like she'd had it. I know my friend and it's easy to tell her mood by the way she walks, by her face, even by the way she stands. She was beat. Even her red hair looked limp. And she brought peanut butter-and-jelly sandwiches on white bread. A last minute lunch. The pits.

"What's wrong, Monique?"

She just shook her head.

For months I had been pouring all my hard luck stories into her ears regularly. Now I wanted her to confide in me. I really wanted to listen to her and to help her. "What is it?"

"Nothing, Carole."

"Come on. Tell me."

"Nothing. I'm your best friend. I tell you everything."

"I don't want to actually say it out loud because once I say it it's more likely to come true than if I only think it."

"Since when are you so superstitious?"

"Since the day I broke the magnifying mirror."

"It's still that guy, Al?"

She nodded.

"Sorry. He's lasted longer than most of Gloria's boyfriends."

"He's going to last longer than you'd believe."

"Look, forget broken mirrors and all that stuff. Tell me what's happening."

She really had to struggle with it. I could see her arguing with herself, yes/no/yes/no, and then it burst out of her and I understood her reluctance to say it. "Gloria says she's going to marry him."

It was totally unexpected and I didn't know how to handle it. "If she's happy, I guess you should be happy for her," I said lamely. Monique was so obviously unhappy; it was a dumb thing to say. I just couldn't think of anything else.

"I don't like him," she said softly, moving closer to me on the lunchroom bench as Christa passed us on her way to another table. Christa barely nodded to me these days. Jean always said hello and smiled as she moved on, but Christa barely acknowledged me with a flick of her eyelids. I had heard she was telling people my family was strange. "He's slick," Monique continued. "Gloria says I have no reason not to like him. He's nice to her. He's nice to me. But you can't like a person just because you're expected to."

"What's wrong with him? I mean now you know him better, so can you explain your feelings? What does he *do* wrong?"

Monique pondered for a while. "He doesn't *do* anything wrong. That's what's driving Gloria crazy. She even thinks I'm jealous. Jealous!" She choked on the thought. "I just don't trust him. I can't say why, but there is something wrong about him. You know how some people are naturally very easygoing? Well, he *seems* easygoing, very laid-back. But that's what I don't trust."

"It's not much to go on, Monique. I don't think you're jealous. That's loony. But you *don't* have much evidence. Is she really thinking of marrying him? When?"

"He wants it now, soon. He's all ready to move in. He hangs around all the time anyway. Every night that they don't go out he comes and sits in front of the television and drinks beer. And he keeps it on so loud! In my room I can hear the dialogue perfectly. There I am

trying to do my homework and I'm listening to basket-
ball or wrestling or 'Hill Street Blues'."

"Ask him to turn it down."

"He's Gloria's guest."

"Ask him politely. Tell him you can't concentrate on
your homework when the TV is playing so loud."

"I don't want to upset Gloria."

"Monique, it's not an unreasonable request. In my
house whoever is watching can't do it at anyone else's
expense. It's courtesy."

"I'll try," she said, but I could tell she didn't have
much hope that it would work.

She did try. Next day she looked even worse so I knew
it hadn't worked. I had packed liverwurst-and-lettuce
on big soft poppy seed rolls and brought along a large
bag of Doritos (nacho flavor, of course), and I was glad
to see her eating away. But she looked glum.

"Okay," I said, "what happened?"

"He turned the TV on, blasting. Would you believe
the roller derby? So I went in and spoke to him very
politely."

"He got mad?"

"No. He never gets mad. He just laughed at me.
'Kid,' he said, 'you have to learn to concentrate because
when you're really concentrating on something you
don't hear anything else.'"

"He really said that to you?"

"There's more. He told me that when he was in
school and did his homework—which wasn't too often

because he was a quick study and not a grind—he always did it watching TV, sometimes two sets at a time if there were two sports events he wanted to catch."

"Who cares what he did? I'm beginning to see what you mean about him. He's got nerve. It's not even his house."

"Yet."

"Didn't Gloria stick up for you?"

"She offered to buy me a Walkman so I can tune the TV out. She's just so crazy about him she can't bear to criticize him."

"What does she see in him?"

"He cheers her up. He's sexy. He's funny. He tells her she's beautiful and she is looking beautiful these days. She's just glowing. After the Jogger went, she was down in the dumps."

"I'm so sorry, Monique."

"If they get married and he comes to live in our house, I don't think I can stand it."

"Maybe you can get Gloria to hold off the wedding till June. That's the big wedding month. Since you're going to be a junior counselor at camp all summer, they can have the whole house to themselves."

Monique grabbed on to that idea and hugged it like a life preserver. "Yes," she said, "June. The month for brides. Gloria would be willing to wait for that. She'll go for it."

Gloria went for it. A June wedding and a whole summer of honeymoon sounded good to her. "Al, dear," she argued, "we've got the rest of our lives. Let's do it right. What's the big hurry?"

"We're not kids," he said. "We don't need to stall around." He continued to be crabby about the idea, but since Gloria was so enthusiastic about a traditional wedding (and hoped Monique would develop a fondness for him), he didn't push it.

Monique was positive he was furious with her.

"It's your imagination," I told her. "If he doesn't say anything wrong or do anything wrong then how can you tell he's angry?"

"I don't know. Vibes. Intuition. I am telling you, Carole, my mother's fiancé is one angry man because his wedding is being postponed, and the person he is angriest at is me. The question is what is he going to do about it?"

"I'm not sure you are right about him being angry. But, just in case, Monique, stay out of his way."

All the while this was going on, I was dusting regularly. Twice each week I showed up in Rhonda's kitchen after track. She fed me brownies and milk, or raisin cookies, or oatmeal cookies, and then sent me into the silent upstairs where for two hours—eternity—I vacuumed the huge Persian rugs and dusted. I never dropped a piece. I never saw anyone but Rhonda.

On our magic blackboard, in English class, the quote of the week was, "When a man knows he's to be hanged . . . it concentrates his mind wonderfully." Dr. Samuel Johnson, the man who put together the first dictionary,

said that in 1777. Well, when a girl has to dust endlessly, it concentrates her mind pretty wonderfully as
well. It's such an idiot job, it leaves you free to focus on
important things, to think.

Those long hours brought back to me all the warnings
I had heard about the importance of school and the
dangers of being unskilled. I'd laughed at Mom and her
word-processing course because we had no word processor at home. Look how handy it was when she
needed a job.

Skills, Gloria had been preaching to Monique and me
for years. Self-reliance. Learn all kinds of things. Life is
tricky. You never know.

Who would have thought Mom would need a job? I
guess that was the area I was most underdeveloped in,
the who-would-have-thought possibilities. That was
what Monique meant when she told me long ago that I
saw my parents—and my life—as predictable.

And even Monique, who had lived with constant
change her whole life, who had been conditioned by
Gloria not to expect any steady course, even Monique
was unprepared for the wild direction her life was veer-
ing in. How could she have anticipated Al?

During those long dusting hours I came to terms
with the reality that who-would-have-thought is a constant in everyone's life.

The single moment of joy on those Tuesday and
Thursday evenings was when on my way out I picked
up the ten-dollar bill Rhonda had waiting. "Enjoy it,"
she said, each time. "You earned it."

I loved hearing it.

Who would have thought Credit-Card Carole would earn her spending money dusting toy soldiers and dishes?

Monique took my advice and did her very best to stay out of Al's way. She baby-sat whenever she could so she wasn't at home so many evenings. But Al occupied the house like a victorious army in a losing country. He was almost always there. For a while they didn't collide because Monique was so extra careful and went tiptoeing around him. So, if he really was angry at her, he couldn't do much about it. She was courteous and elusive.

Then he did something about it. Or, at least we were convinced that he did. Something remarkably vicious.

Monique left an essay she had written for English on Gloria's desk for Gloria to read. The essay was about Gloria's wonderful sense of color and style and how her bold and original use of color brightened their home and their lives. Monique spent three hours of prime time writing that essay; she did it while baby-sitting in a house that had cable and HBO. She never went near the tube. She just wrote all night. Things hadn't been good between her and Gloria since Al was always around, and she wanted Gloria to know how proud she was of her.

The loving couple was in the living room when Monique came home about midnight. So she went in to say good-night to them. "I left something personal on your desk for you to read," she told Gloria, "later." Then she went upstairs.

About ten minutes later, she heard Gloria calling her and she knew something bad had happened. She ran downstairs and there on the sink drainboard was her essay soggy with beer and her mother contrite and frantic and Al very apologetic. Very, very apologetic. After Gloria read it and said it was so good, she had put it back on the desk, and he had decided he wanted to read it. So, he'd gone over and set his can of Heineken's down and then accidentally knocked it over.

"I meant for my mother to read it," Monique said. "It was a personal essay about her."

"I said I was sorry, kid. I didn't see any harm in my reading it. Your teacher is going to read it. And after all, I'm practically your father."

Monique was dying to tell him that in no way was he practically her father and that it was none of his business, but Gloria was so pale and edgy, dabbling at the running ink and saying maybe it could be saved, maybe it could be photocopied. The pages were soaked.

"It's all right, Gloria," Monique said. "I can recopy it. I just need a quiet place."

Al took the hint and left. Then Monique had to calm Gloria and talk her into going to bed. When the place was quiet, she sat down at her mother's desk and did a new copy. It took her until almost two o'clock.

114

The spilled beer was an open declaration of war. As she wrote, Monique made up her mind resolutely.

"I'm not going to let him win," she told me. "He's not going to marry my mother."

"How will you stop him?"

"I'll find a way. I have to!"

CHAPTER 16

Things were really sticky at the Dunhams'. I knew about it because Rhonda asked me secretly if I couldn't get Jim to go and buy some new clothes—just jeans and stuff, nothing fancy—because his father was furious with him for going around in rags. He wouldn't allow him into the dining room to eat at the dinner table. "Your costume is an offense to my eyes," he told Jim. Rhonda was very troubled, but if I knew Jim he was probably much happier in the kitchen. However, that wasn't the point.

"Rhonda, you know when Jim makes up his mind, nothing moves him. He doesn't want new clothes. He doesn't want to spend his father's money."

Rhonda sighed. "You're right. But Mr. Dunham is on

116

the warpath. He's not going to change his mind either. He won't allow his son to go around looking like a bum. They argue all the time."

I couldn't butt in. I just couldn't. I figure you have to respect your friends and support them. I knew how important it was to Jim to go his own way. I also knew there had to be an end to all of this. It couldn't continue.

Mrs. Dunham was out of it; since she was not well, they did their quarreling out of her presence. Jim explained to her that he took dinner in the kitchen because he was busy with schoolwork and had to eat at odd hours. When father and son confronted one another, they took it up to the museum, Rhonda said. "They go up there to his War Room. At least it's good for something besides gathering dust."

One Thursday afternoon, something very strange occurred. Jim was there, at home, when I arrived to do the dusting. By agreement, he had never been around during my work hours before. We had decided that it would be best if when I was working, I was not distracted.

But there he was, sitting in Rhonda's sparkling bright kitchen, skinny, absolutely gaunt, his jeans and shirt literally rags. Worse, he'd had his head shaved. No more beautiful soft blond hair. "Hi, Carole," he said, as if it wasn't extraordinary that he should be sitting there bald as an egg.

"What happened to your hair?"

He shrugged. "Saves haircuts." Behind him, Rhonda shrugged too, mightily.

"Milk and cookies for my favorite children," she said, setting the food out for us. Jim drank the milk but passed on the brownies even though she pushed the dish closer to him. She quickly refilled his glass. "No more," he said. "Thanks."

"How come you're here?" I asked. "You're usually practicing the cello."

"I've given it up."

"You've what?"

"I've given up playing the cello."

"Why?"

"I'm against expensive personal hobbies."

"It wasn't just a hobby. The cello is very important to you. Jim, you're a fine musician. Some day you'll be great. You might win—"

He smiled at me. "Airhead. They don't give the Nobel Prize for music. I told you that."

"Some other great prize then."

"My father's son does not become a professional musician. My father's son does not consider going to Juilliard or any music conservatory."

"What are you raving about?"

"My father's son aims to be a man of consequence. A doer."

"Your father made you give up the cello?"

"No. He said to cultivate it as a hobby. A cultural experience. Like Mother's porcelains and his soldiers."

118

"So, for now while you're in high school it's a hobby. Later on you can do what you want. Your playing is gorgeous. You could become a great musician."

He was shaking his head. I felt like crying for his lost hair and his rags and everything. His life was a disaster! "Jim, remember after the last school concert? Mr. Santini said your playing was brilliant. Brilliant! Nobody ever said my running was brilliant, but I wouldn't give it up for anything."

"The maestro was very kind," Jim said. Absent-mindedly he drank the second glass of milk. Rhonda, behind him, watched triumphantly; I guess she was practically force-feeding him these days. "But what does he know? As my father said, 'He's only a high school music teacher. That's where his talent got him.'"

"This is too much for me. I better go dust, or I'll be here very late."

"Keep your ears open, Carole. Dusting might not be so boring tonight." His smile was bitter. Rhonda just stood there looking bleak.

I had done all the military miniatures, and I'd vacuumed the rugs in both rooms. I was working on the platters on the wide upper shelves when I heard their voices next door. I was not sure exactly what I should do. Jim knew I was there. I doubted that his father knew it because Mr. Dunham would never have a family quarrel in public; he was very proud. And discreet. So, in a way I was an eavesdropper and in a way not.

119

Since they had come up the stairs already arguing, there was no way I could make my presence known without causing embarrassment. I just kept dusting holding tight to each object. This was not the night to drop anything, not even the dustcloth.

"You look like a convict," Mr. Dunham was saying. "An escapee. What could have possessed you to do such a thing?"

"It's quick and cheap. They do it with a razor. I have something to tell you."

"I see you are still in those clothes." Mr. Dunham's voice was contained but harsh.

"They're my clothes."

"What are you trying to prove, James?"

"Nothing. The haircut and the clothes are not important. I have something I want to tell you if you'll let me."

"All right. What is it?"

"You know my cello?"

"Of course I know your cello. Mother and I bought it for you on your fourteenth birthday. In those days you had hair and dressed relatively normally. There were problems, but I look back on that time as a happier one."

"You did give it to me as a gift?"

"Of course we did."

"I've sold it."

I nearly dropped the Limoges cake plate I was dusting. There was a long silence.

"You've sold the cello? Why?"

"I got fifteen hundred dollars for it. I contributed the money to help fight apartheid. There's a campaign going on in our school."

Mr. Dunham didn't say anything for a while. When he spoke, his voice was hoarse. "You loved that instrument. James, you've lost your reason."

"Yes, I loved it. But I found my reason, I didn't lose it."

"Why? Why did you do it?"

"I wanted to contribute something more meaningful than my name on a petition or my applause at a rally."

"You are not responsible for the evils of the world," his father said slowly. "And individuals do not change the world."

"I have to do what I think is right."

"James, you loved that cello. Just listen. You could have asked me for a contribution. I would have been glad—"

Jim was frantic. "No! I didn't want *your* contribution. *I* wanted to contribute. And—I know just what you're about to say. I don't want you to buy back that cello, and I don't want another, even better cello! If you want to do something, contribute some money yourself. There's a girl in school, Angie Samuels, heading the drive. You want to help alleviate suffering in South Africa? Give it to Angie, directly. Not to me to give to her. Give it openly. Or would you rather not contribute openly?"

"I will send her a contribution," Mr. Dunham said quietly. "Human tragedy and suffering does not please me though you seem to think that it does." He stopped and blew his nose. "But you and I are not able to talk to one another. We will never be able to share our lives. That is our private tragedy."

"It's not my fault."

"Nor is it mine, James. I did not make this world, and I am not responsible for its inequities. Each one of us must do the best he can with his life."

"I'm trying." Jim's voice had a quaver. When he wasn't boiling mad, he was very unsure.

"I know that you are. For your honesty of conscience, I have great respect. Most men never experience it. But you are very young, James, and your judgment is poor. Your judgment is faulty."

Jim didn't answer him. The thing he hated to be accused of most was being too young. I held my breath; from the next room, I could sense the tension between them.

"For your mother's sake will you throw away those rags and get some wearable clothing? She misses you terribly at table. Most often, dinner with you—and me—was the point of her day."

Jim broke down. "All right. I'll get some jeans and shirts."

"And shoes and socks too, please. Running shoes will do. Has she seen your—baldness?"

"Not yet."

"Please give her some reason for it. Tell her it's a new teenage fashion. Tell her you lost a bet. Something, anything. She needs your love, James. She needs *you*."

"Okay," Jim said, "okay."

Their footsteps receded. It was an uneasy truce, but at least it was a truce.

CHAPTER
17

Suddenly, without any warning, Gloria's boyfriend decided it was time to take a walk. That was how he put it. Actually, very little walking was involved. He drove up in the afternoon, all dressed up in his leather coat, and he told Gloria it was time for him to take a walk.

Monique was up in her room when she heard her mother's voice, very upset.

"What are you talking about?" Gloria asked. "What about the wedding in June? What about all of our plans?"

"Oh, baby, I told you that June was too far away. Something came up and I have to move on. It's been fun."

"Al"—Gloria lowered her voice, but Monique had

her door open and she could hear—"what about the money I lent you?"

"I'll send it to you. I'm good for it. You know that."

"I don't know anything of the kind. I lent you that money because you had a business emergency. And because we were going to build a life together. Now you're going off. I can't afford to lose three thousand dollars."

Monique gasped.

"That money came from a special savings account that I never touch."

Monique knew it was the account her mother had started so that she could go to college. It was their only special account.

Al's voice took on a nasty edge. First time, Monique said, that he had dropped the phony, always good-natured front. "Listen," he said, "I could have walked without saying good-bye. I could have done you dirt, just disappeared. But I'm a gentleman. I came to tell you straight. When I'm in the money, you get it all back. But not before then, obviously. And not if you do any complaining to the police."

"And if you're never *in the money?*"

Monique heard the old easy laugh that was his trademark. "That's negative thinking, Gloria, honey. It won't take you anywhere."

"Where are you going?"

"Away. It's been fun. Bye."

And, just like that, he slammed the door. A minute

later they heard him gunning the motor of his cream Alfa Romeo, and he was gone. Monique, watching through her window, felt intense relief. She could hear her mother sobbing in the downstairs hall. She hurried down. "I overheard, Mom. I'm so sorry."

Gloria was despairing and, at the same time, furious with herself. "How could I have been so dumb? How could I have done it?" she asked herself over and over. "How? I'm not a naive kid. How?"

"Mom, it could have happened to anyone."

"No." Gloria denied it. "No, it couldn't. It could only happen to me. You don't know the worst of it, honey."

"I think I do. He 'walked' with my money for college."

Gloria grabbed her and hugged her and kept telling her how sorry she was. Monique did her best to calm her mother down. It took a long time. And when Gloria had finally quieted down and washed her face with cold water, Monique said, "I'm glad he's gone. I never trusted him, and I was so scared for you, so scared he would hurt you. He purposely spilled that beer on my essay about you. He was mean."

Gloria just sat there, numb.

"Some day a nice man will come along, Mom, and he'll appreciate you."

Gloria let the "Mom" go by without protest. She even managed a shaky try at a smile. "I need a written guarantee. I don't think I can wait, on speculation, much longer."

Monique was encouraged. It was a Tough Gloria kind

of line, and it meant she was trying to handle the dirty serve that had been dealt her.

My parents had, in the past months, proven to be unknown quantities. Now Gloria—whom Monique knew to be unpredictable—surprised and scared *her*, terribly. She thought Gloria was strong enough to handle anything. Even Al's walking off with three thousand dollars. Gloria was subdued during the following few days, but she was functioning, going about her business. She even talked about getting extra work, so they could recoup their loss. She knew she had been taken. *Al*fa Romeo (her joke) was gone for good.

However, it must suddenly have hit her hard because when Monique came in from school late one afternoon she found Gloria lying in bed and the telephone answering machine still taking messages. Gloria was not awake, and, apparently, had not been up all day.

For Gloria, this was freaky behavior. She's remarkably energetic. She runs her own business and does aerobics and belongs to every service organization in town. The Ashland Chamber of Commerce gave her a plaque for public service. She goes to bed late and gets up early. She runs on what she calls nervous energy.

"Gloria? You okay? You sick?" Monique kept talking but she couldn't rouse her. She shook her. She dashed cold water in her face. Then she began to get real scared and she called our house.

"No one's here but me," I told her, "and I'll be right over. But you better get an adult."

"Who?"

"The Jogger!" we both said together.

Luckily he was in. He came fast, and he took one look at Gloria and saw she was limp, absolutely out of it. He took her pulse, and then he grabbed the phone. "She'll be okay if we can get help fast, Monique," he said, and he called the Ashland police. An ambulance would be along in minutes.

"What is it?" Monique asked him. "What's wrong?"

The Jogger wasn't sure. "Does she ever take sleeping pills?"

"Once in a while when she's all keyed up. Or depressed. She doesn't like to take them. But they never do this to her."

"Maybe she made a mistake and took one too many. Or a wrong combination. We'll have to wait and see."

The ambulance people were fast. They were so skillful you wouldn't believe they were just everyday townspeople who were volunteers. Angie Samuels's father, who owns one of the small local gas stations, brought in the stretcher. I knew him from our track meets. He's about six feet five inches tall, an immense silent man. I've never heard him yell, not even when Angie came in first—as she often did. At tight moments he'd just smile and raise his fists high in the air and shake them till she made it.

Now he nodded to me and he and the other two attendants wrapped Gloria in a blanket and took her out.

When I'm old enough, I'm going to join the ambulance corps. I might even suggest it to Jim; he's almost old enough now. *There's* something good he can *do*. Why didn't I think of it before?

The ambulance took off for the county hospital. Monique, the Jogger, and I followed in his car. Gloria got checked into the hospital okay, and the nurse said there was no use our hanging around there. They would phone us as soon as she came to or they knew anything. The Jogger said he would hang around anyway, but first he'd drive us to my house. "Monique can stay there with me as long as she wants to," I said. I knew it would be okay.

Once he left us at home, we didn't talk. Our minds were back there in the hospital with Gloria and whatever was happening to her. I kept thinking about how young she looked without any makeup, how much like Monique. How lovely.

The Jogger kept us posted. By six o'clock that evening the hospital had Gloria awake, her stomach pumped. She *had* made a mistake with her sleeping pills, and she was very groggy now but she was going to be fine.

Mom was not back from work yet and Daddy wasn't home either; he was still being Bogie (and beginning to worry about what would come next); it was almost the end of the play's run and he had loved every second of it.

"Take a taxi to the hospital," the Jogger said. "I'll be waiting downstairs to pay for it."

We did, and he was. One thing I have to say about runners, even joggers. They're sincere.

It was a semiprivate room, but the other bed was empty. Gloria was lying on her back covered by a thin white hospital blanket. Her face was pale and her hair very red in all that whiteness. She stirred slightly at the sound of the door, but she seemed to be dozing. The Jogger went up to the bed and stood there a while watching her intently. "Gloria?" he said, and then he bent over and said it again in her ear, several times more. "Gloria?"

She mumbled something but still didn't open her eyes. Then, suddenly, she said clearly, "What time is it?"

"It's six-thirty at night," Monique told her.

"Six-thirty?" Gloria opened her eyes and tried to lift her head, but she was weak. She just lay back, her eyes fully opened now. "I'm dreaming," she said.

"No, you're not. It's me, Harold. The Jogger."

"Why are you here?" She looked around. "Where is here? Where are we anyhow?"

"In the county hospital, Gloria," Monique said. "Harold and Carole and I brought you here." She stopped, and then went on in a much lower voice. "You made a mistake with your sleeping pills."

Gloria shifted her eyes away from us. She looked at her hands on the blanket.

"Let's leave Monique and her mother for a bit," the

130

Jogger suggested, taking me by the hand. "We'll go downstairs and get some refreshments."

He bought me a double-scoop strawberry ice cream soda at the snack bar in the basement. He was very interested in my running, the only adult I ever met other than our coach who was really interested in the girls' running team. I mean, my parents and Larry are interested too, but that's because I'm on the team. The Jogger cared about the sport!

This Jogger was a prince, a king, a nobleman at the very least. Gloria had not recognized his true worth. As I drank pink soda and we talked, I made up my mind to start a propaganda blitz in favor of the Jogger. So his hair was a little thin and his sweats weren't designer-made. He was a million, a trillion times better than any of Gloria's other boyfriends. A zillion times better than Al!

The Jogger didn't know it, but in me he had just found a powerful friend.

When we went back upstairs, Monique was sitting close to the bed talking to her mother.

Gloria smiled. "Monique's been telling me how you guys came through. I want to thank you."

"A pleasure," the Jogger said. "I was just waiting for one of my two favorite redheads to call me up."

"I'm in your debt," Gloria said, a little embarrassed. Perhaps she was remembering the restaurant and the pack of cigarettes and her bad manners.

131

"You can pay it off by coming jogging. It's no fun alone after those mornings with you ladies. Remember the time we met the skunk?"

"And you outstared him?" Monique giggled. "That was fantastic."

"Not outstared. Hypnotized," he said immodestly. He looked directly at Gloria. "We'd have to work on your breathing," he said. "Smoking damages it."

"Don't you ever give up?" Gloria teased him.

"No. Not on important things."

She reached a hand out to him and he grasped it. "I am going to take a page from your book," she said. "I am never, never, never going to give up. No matter what." She looked at Monique. "I was stupid about a lot of things. But I'm going to work at being smarter. Anyone with a daughter like Monique has too much to live for to ever do anything dumb." She winked at Monique. "You don't have to worry, honey. I am never going to take a walk."

"But you will run often with me," the Jogger said, "because that's really the only way to go."

Gloria sighed, a great, dramatic, overdone sigh. "What are you going to do with these guys who never give up?"

Monique and I walked out leaving the Jogger to take care of that big question.

CHAPTER
18

Big family conference brought about by a confluence of
events. Nice word, confluence; it means flowing together and the word itself has a flowing sound. One
thing Brutal Blake taught me in this term's English
class is to love words. He's so nutty about it, it's catch-
ing. Learn them and use them, he says. Adopt them
and make them your own. Confluence is mine now but
I don't think I'll get much chance to use it. If it were a
verb I could say to Monique, "Let's confluent tonight
and go for a soda." But it's a noun and Blake says you
can't take words and torture them that way. That's
called a "back-formation" and to English teachers it's
the prime crime.

I didn't realize I'd learned so much this term. My
mind has certainly been on other things. I guess there

is something to be said for mandatory attendance even though some days the body sits there and the mind travels. Learning by absorbing. Osmosis! Another gem.

Back to the conference brought on by the confluence.

Larry hitchhiked in from school for the weekend. I looked him over very critically, and he really isn't bad looking. He's dark-haired and has good features; he's my dad grown tall. I was still pretty impressed that he modeled for art students and the school *paid him* to do it. I mean—my brother! Who would want to draw him? A lot of people, apparently, or so he claimed. According to him the mailman brought millions of mash notes from girls in the sketch classes, but he never mixed business with pleasure. He was supporting himself okay that way. Next year he would apply for a student loan, but the way he figured it he was in good shape. Many of his classmates were already deeply in debt having taken loans from the very beginning.

It was nice to have him around again even if he was the same old tease. First thing he said, starting out real nice and friendly, was, "Carole, you're making real progress—toward becoming a human being." And, later, after I'd put my eye makeup on, he asked if I was going out to play baseball. "No," I said. "You know I don't play baseball. I run."

"It's an honest mistake, Carole. With all that black grease on your cheeks, I thought you were made up for the glare on the ballfield."

Brothers!

But he did come with me over to the high school

track on Saturday afternoon, and he watched me run and clocked me and he was very enthusiastic. "Work on your start, kid," he said. "Stay under control and you'll be college scholarship material." He really meant it.

The topic of our family conference was: What Do We Do Next? It was held Sunday evening after an overwhelming dinner of Cantonese duck (made with apricot glaze!) and wild rice and asparagus, and mocha layer cake, Larry's favorite nonsweet in the world. When he eats too much of it and Mom warns him about sweets, he always says mocha is a nonsweet. Since he doesn't get home from school so often, the feast was in his honor.

While we were sitting around afterward, stuffed and contented, Daddy put it to us. He had to make a decision, but it was not really his to make. *Play It Again, Sam* was over. It had had rave notices and a good run. "I'm already ahead," Daddy said. "I haven't had such a good time in years. In my whole life. The question is what do I do now? I'm jobless again."

Mom didn't even have to think about it. "As for me," she said, "I like my own job very much. Even if you went back to dentistry tomorrow, I would stay where I am. Mr. Button-Down Campbell and Ms. Violet Mudd are beginning to regard me as the elder stateswoman of commerce. Because I can spell and write grammatical sentences and because I have a little common sense, they defer to me. I love it."

"Dad, I think you should go for it," Larry said. "*Sam* was only the beginning. I mean—one show. As far as

I'm concerned, I'm doing okay. I like being the model for the multitudes. It's real good exposure." He waited for his laugh so we gave it to him. "So you don't have to go back to full-time dentistry ever as far as I'm concerned."

"Two accounted for," Daddy said. "That leaves you, Carole. In a way, since you're the youngest and most dependent, you've been hit the hardest by this change. Whatever I decide affects your life tremendously. I remember how badly you felt when we cut up your credit card. End of the world. We do have some money set aside for college for you, but you will have to help yourself. So, answer as honestly as you can. If it were left up to you, right this minute, what would you tell me to do? Consider carefully and don't answer for anyone else, not for Larry or Mom or me. Answer for Carole."

It wasn't hard. "Daddy, you're a terrific actor," I began. "Maybe you're a terrific dentist too, but no one else can see inside your patients' mouths. It's just no contest. You belong on the stage."

"Remember how they pay actors, kid. You may never get another credit card. And I may not make it into the big time."

"When you're onstage, you are big time," I said sincerely.

"I said it before, but I have to say it again," Daddy started solemnly, "I've got the crucial ingredient. No matter what happens I am supremely armored. This family is my shield against all the slings and arrows of outrageous fortune."

"*Hamlet?* The To-be-or-not-to-be speech?" Larry said quickly.

"You beat me to it," I said. He sure did. I didn't recognize the line.

Mom was looking at Daddy fondly. "Aren't you being a bit dramatic?" she asked.

"Thank you," he said, and gave a deep curtain-call bow, the kind that precedes an encore.